FOLK TALES AND FAIRY STORIES FROM INDIA

SUDHIN N. GHOSE

DOVER PUBLICATIONS, INC.
Mineola, New York

Bibliographical Note

This Dover edition, first published in 1996, contains only the text of the work originally published by The Golden Cockerel Press, London, 1961, in an edition limited to 500 numbered copies. All of the original illustrations and references to the illustrator have been omitted from the Dover edition.

Library of Congress Cataloging-in-Publication Data

Ghose, Sudhindra Nath.
    Folk tales and fairy stories from India / Sudhin N. Ghose.
        p.   cm.
    Originally published: London : Golden Cockerel Press, 1961. With new ack.
    ISBN 0-486-29247-9 (pbk.)
    1. Tales—India.   2. Fairy tales—India.   I. Title.
GR308.G45   1996
398.2'0954—dc20   96–17770
                                                            CIP

Manufactured in the United States of America
Dover Publications, Inc., 31 East 2nd Street, Mineola, N.Y. 11501

For

Bisaskha, Jaya, Manzu, Naz, and Subhankar

" . . . Should enchantment cease
A forest dead and dry the world would be."
Bhavabhuti

ACKNOWLEDGMENTS

The repertory of Indian folk tales and fairy stories is so vast and varied that it is impossible to make a truly representative selection within the compass of a single volume. My task has, however, been considerably simplified for I have been guided in my choice by the likes and the dislikes of a number of eminent Indologists.

Grateful acknowledgments are due to the memory of the following: Alfred Foucher, Ishwan Chandra Ghosh, René Grousset, Sylvain Lévi, Sir John Malcolm, Raja Rajendra Lal Mitra, Arthur W. Ryder, and Sir Monier Monier-Williams; short excerpts from their renderings of the Jatakas, the Avadanas, the Katha-Sarit-Sagara, and other works have been incorporated in some of the stories in the present selection.

Cordial thanks are tendered to the undermentioned for reading the MS. of this book and offering suggestions: Allan M. Laing, Ray Palmer, R. Watson, E. M. Weiser, and E. Carlile.

S.N.G.

CONTENTS

Palwahn the Wrestler

THERE ONCE WAS A YOUNG wrestler, called Palwahn, who was known to be a hot-head. 'I am not a bit afraid of demons,' he declared one day in the middle of the market place. 'As for gnomes and goblins,' he kept on, 'I am ready to play ball with them.'

'What about the ghouls?' the villagers asked as they crowded round him. 'Can you face the ones infesting the Valley of Wrath?'

'What are they like?' Palwahn asked in his turn. 'And tell me, what's funny about the Valley of Wrath?'

'There's nothing funny whatsoever about the Valley,' they replied. 'Surely you know what it is like. It's the barren tract between Dustipore and Bustigunj.'

Palwahn murmured that he had a vague idea of the where-abouts of one of the two towns, Dustipore and Bustigunj, but had not the faintest notion of the ghoul-infested Valley.

'The road linking the two towns,' they explained, 'passes through the Valley.' 'It isn't much of a road,' someone added, 'for it is rugged and broken. It winds through most frightful precipices and deep ravines, and at places it tunnels its way through overhanging crags which shed boulders on all passers-by.'

'That's fine,' Palwahn exclaimed. 'To use that road would be like swimming across a river full of man-eating turtles and cattle-gobbling crocodiles. Turtles and crocodiles don't fright-en me, and there's no reason why the boulders should.'

'But,' the villagers said, 'you have heard only half of the story.' They then made it clear to him that though the natural dangers in the Valley were great enough they were nothing compared with the supernatural ones—the infernal ghouls who lived there. 'The ghouls,' they went on, 'are horrid creatures that feed on carcasses. They waylay travellers and kill them.

And the main trouble with them is that they can assume any shape they choose to mislead the unwary.'

'When passing through the Valley,' a mango-seller began, 'you may come across a cow or a camel, and you may well wonder, "What's that cow doing here?" or "Whose camel can it possibly be?" But before you have done with your wondering the cow or the camel will change into a giant to knock you down.' 'Maybe,' a melon-vendor added, 'the animal will take the shape of one of your friends and ask for a drink of water, and then suddenly turn into a vampire to suck the last drop of blood out of you.'

'In other words,' Palwahn interrupted the villagers, 'you don't know what a ghoul looks like. That's the plain truth. Well, I am off to the Valley of Wrath this very minute. When I come back you will hear more about your famous carcass-eaters.'

'Don't be silly,' they all cried. 'It would be sheer madness to venture into the Valley all by yourself.'

But Palwahn refused to be dissuaded. Being a hothead he lost his temper altogether when the whole village wailed, 'You are only a middling good wrestler: how will you tackle a ghoul?'

'Never mind how: I'll do it,' Palwahn growled. 'I'll make a fool of the first ghoul I come across.' He swore roundly as he hurried out of the village taking nothing with him save a small packet which a kind widow thrust into his pocket.

This tiny parcel contained a lump of salt and an egg.

Palwahn smiled when he examined the widow's gifts. For this good lady was known for her eccentricity. She fed her hens with red lentils, red beetroots, and other curious feeding stuffs to get eggs with red yolk. 'I ought to have thanked her,' Palwahn sighed. 'She is the mother of the prettiest girl of the village. Now, however, it is too late; for I am already in the Valley of Wrath.'

Just then he heard a voice calling him by name from a great

distance. 'Friend Palwahn!' the voice quavered, 'You are going the wrong way. You will get lost. I am your friend Doolal. Come this way!'

Palwahn realised at once that the creature that was calling out to him was no other than a ghoul. He was immediately on his guard. However, pretending to be unconcerned he shouted back, 'Where are you, my dear Doolal? It is getting dark and I can't see far. Come near me, and show me the way.'

And soon the ghoul, disguised as Doolal, was by his side.

'Aha!' said Palwahn. 'So here you are! My dear ghoul, I know you: you are a lying rascal, pretending to be Doolal. Anyway, I am lucky. For you are just the creature I was longing to meet. And you know the reason why.'

'Really, I don't,' replied the ghoul, greatly surprised at Palwahn's boldness. Rarely had he met a solitary wayfarer who did not tremble at the mere mention of the word 'ghoul,' and here was Palwahn beaming with delight and declaring that he was lucky! It didn't make much sense. So he repeated, 'Really, I don't know why you have been longing to meet me.'

'That proves,' Palwahn snapped, 'you are a stupid ghoul. You can't read a man's thoughts. So you must be pretty worthless. However, even a stupid and worthless ghoul is better than no ghoul. Therefore you are welcome. As for me,' he went on, 'I am a champion wrestler. I can easily strangle a cattle-gobbling crocodile, beat a man-eating turtle into jelly, and do many other things of this kind. But to tell the truth, I am sick of trying my strength on natural creatures. I want a supernatural being to fight with. Now do you understand why I am in this Valley all alone?'

Palwahn's patter made the ghoul speechless. He scrutinized our village wrestler carefully and finally said, 'Well, between ourselves, you don't appear to be so very strong.'

'Appearances are misleading,' Palwahn replied readily. 'Take your case. You appear to be Doolal, but that does not prevent your being a rascally ghoul. Now let me give you a definite proof of my argument and of my strength as well.

There,' he said, picking up a piece of rock from the ground, 'take this stone and feel it. It appears to be dead and dry. But I tell you it is filled with a fluid. Squeeze it hard and see for yourself if I am right or wrong.'

The ghoul took the stone and did his best to squeeze it, but after a short attempt returned it, saying, 'It is impossible.'

'Quite easy,' said Palwahn, putting the stone into his pocket and then taking it out again with the widow's egg. 'Look here! See the blood of the stone oozing out because I have pressed it hard!'

The cracking of the egg made just enough noise to create the illusion that the stone was being crushed, and then the red yolk running through Palwahn's fingers proved his point: 'Appearances are deceptive.'

The ghoul was too astonished to notice how Palwahn got rid of his broken egg-shell as well as of the stone while picking up a pebble of a dark colour.

'Here,' Palwahn said, 'here is something to prove further my strength, and what's more, my power of seeing through things. Take this dark pebble and tell me what you see.'

The ghoul took it and after peering at it for a minute declared that he was no good at seeing things in the dark: the evening was already far advanced. But so far as he was concerned the pebble in question was a pebble and nothing more.

'So,' Palwahn sneered, 'you are as good as night-blind. True it has become dark, but not so dark as to hide the qualities of this pebble. This, let me assure you, contains salt. Just crumble it between your fingers, and you will see what happens.'

The ghoul looked at it again and tried his strength on it and finally confessed that he had neither the gift of discovering its qualities nor the power of breaking it between his fingers.

'That's a shame,' Palwahn remarked. 'Give it back to me. I thought I was lucky when you greeted me, but now I know I am not really lucky. What's the use of challenging a weakling like you to a wrestling match in the dark? You will be floored in a minute.' He went on talking in this way while he dropped the pebble into his pocket and took out the lump of salt he had received from the eccentric widow. 'Now,' he said as he crushed the lump between his fingers, 'now taste the powdered pebble and tell me if it contains salt or not.'

The ghoul did as he was told and became alarmed: Palwahn was right. What would happen, he asked himself, should the wonderful man exert his strength on him? There was no possibility of escape by changing his form into that of a beast. For Palwahn had warned him that if he started any such unfair dealing he would receive no mercy: he would be instantly slain by our village wrestler. 'Between ourselves,' Palwahn had remarked a few minutes earlier, 'I know ghouls are not, after all, immortal, and even if you were, I should like to take you back with me to my village as my prisoner. My friends have never seen a ghoul and it would certainly be amusing for them to inspect you. But I believe in fair play. As you can't see well in the dark I have no intention of fighting you tonight.' In the circumstances, the ghoul thought, the best plan would be to win the wrestler's confidence, take him home and see that he got to bed soon. 'Then,' he said to himself, 'I shall smash him to smithereens.'

So he started talking to Palwahn in an ingratiating way.

'Sir,' he said, 'I know of ghouls who would be only too willing to be taken into captivity by a valiant wrestler like you. I know of others who would be your worthy match. But as for me, I am too insignificant a member of my tribe to deserve your attention. All the same,' he continued, 'since providence has given me the opportunity of meeting you, may I request you to honour my humble residence with your presence? It is quite near. And in my home you will find every comfort and refreshment. After a pleasant night's rest you may resume your journey, and on your way back pick up as many ghouls as you wish to take with you to your village.'

'Friend ghoul,' Palwahn replied, 'I have no objection to your proposal. But mind you, I am a short-tempered man. I brook no disrespectful word. Moreover, I can read people's thoughts as clearly as I can see salt or blood hidden inside rocks. So take care that you harbour no wicked designs, nor use any foul language in my presence.'

At this the ghoul swore by the head of the Chief of his tribe that Palwahn's conditions were accepted and the laws of hospitality would be scrupulously respected. Then he led our wrestler through a number of crooked paths and narrow gullies to a large cave, which was lit by innumerable shining gems and luminous precious stones. 'Here, sir,' he declared, 'is my humble abode. Though poor it will furnish you with all you want for refreshment and repose. Let me now show you round my various apartments.'

Though the entrance to the cave was nothing spectacular and rather narrow, it led to spacious galleries hollowed out of a cliff. There were large rooms filled to overflowing with every species of grain and all sorts of merchandise, the accumulated wealth of plundered caravans. There were also ample signs— bleached bones, for instance—to inform Palwahn that the ghoul did subsist on the carcasses of travellers deluded or dragged into his den.

'Will this be sufficient for your honour's supper?' the ghoul asked Palwahn as he took up a bag of rice as big as a barge. 'A man of your strength must have a corresponding appetite.'

'True,' said Palwahn. 'But I am a professional wrestler, and my trainer taught me to be moderate. I live virtually on one meal a day, and that is pretty modest: only one whole sheep and a bag of rice of about the size you have just taken up. But I had my meal before starting on my journey. So I don't really need anything for tonight. However, for your sake—to keep the laws of hospitality and friendship—I shall take a handful of rice. Only a handful.'

'I must boil it for you,' said the ghoul. 'For surely you do not relish grain or meat raw like me. Here is a cooking pan,' he continued as he fished out one from a heap of plundered property. 'And I will now go and get some wood and light a fire in the kitchen, while you might perhaps fetch some water with that.' A gigantic leather bottle was pointed out to Palwahn: it was made of the hide of several oxen.

Our wrestler waited till his host had gone out to fetch some firewood. He then tried to drag the monstrous leather bottle, or bag, to a fountain in a corner of the cave. With great difficulty he managed to trundle it some distance and then the thought struck him, how was he to take it to the kitchen when filled with water. 'I can hardly manage it when empty,' he said to himself. 'It would demand a hundred like me to carry it when full.'

So he decided that it would be easier to carve a runnel across the floor, from the fountain to the kitchen, and picked up an instrument resembling a shovel, edged with sharp diamonds. His idea was not at all bad, and the instrument sufficiently sharp to cut stone. But it was a time-taking job to scoop out a runnel of a hundred feet or thereabouts—the distance between the fountain and the kitchen. In an hour's time he managed only a couple of feet.

'What are you doing there?' roared the ghoul when he found Palwahn busy with his shovel. 'I ask you to bring a drop of water to boil a handful of rice, and you have been about it for an age. Can't you fill the leather bottle and bring it away?'

'Certainly, I can,' Palwahn replied. 'Not only one bottle but a dozen, if I were content to give a show of my brute strength. But that would be a poor way of manifesting my liking for you. But here,' he continued, pointing to the channel he had started for conducting the water of the fountain, 'here is the beginning of something of permanent interest, a sound token of my appreciation of your hospitality. This canal, though slender, will when completed bring water to your kitchen. It will spare you the bother of moving to and fro with that uncouth leather bottle. But please leave me alone till it is finished. I shall work on it all night, if necessary.'

'Nonsense,' growled the ghoul impatiently, as he seized the leather bag and filled it. 'I will carry the water myself. And it would be against all laws of hospitality if I allowed you to remain awake all night. You must go to bed as soon as you have finished your supper. Toil on your canal tomorrow all day if you like.'

Palwahn congratulated himself on his narrow escape, and readily followed his host to the kitchen. He had a hearty meal and then went to repose on a bed made of the richest coverlets and pillows taken out of one of the store-rooms of plundered goods. However, though the bed was most comfortable it was impossible for him to fall asleep. Terror and anxiety kept him awake.

But as for the ghoul, no sooner had he laid himself down than he fell fast asleep and ere long began to snore peacefully. Now Palwahn got up gently and stuffed a long bolster in the middle of his bed to make it appear as though he were still there; he then tiptoed to a corner to hide himself behind a tapestry and watch from there the ghoul's proceedings. The latter woke up with the sunrise and then softly went towards the bed of his guest, carrying in his hand a staff as massive as the main mast of a big boat, and with this he struck a terrible blow on what he thought to be Palwahn's head. And not hearing the least groan, the ghoul smiled, thinking that he had deprived his guest of his life. But to make sure of his end, he struck six more blows, each as formidable as the first one. Then satisfied with his work he returned to his couch and covering his head with his bed sheet settled himself to sleep again.

Palwahn now crept back to his bed and pushed away the bolster and raising his head cried out, 'Friend Ghoul! What strange insects do you breed in your cave? A bug woke me up with its flappings. I counted its seven flappings. Of course it has neither bitten me nor harmed me in any way. Still it is most annoying.'

The ghoul's fright at hearing Palwahn speak at all was great, but it turned to panic when he heard his seven mightiest blows referred to as seven flaps of a mere insect's wings. 'There is no safety,' he said to himself, 'near so formidable a wrestler.' So without uttering a word he jumped up and fled from the cave, leaving Palwahn its sole master.

It needed a string of hired camels from Dustipore and several teams of requisitioned mules from Bustigunj to remove the property Palwahn had acquired. After making restitution to such caravan-owners as were still alive to identify their goods, there was enough left to make him a man of great wealth.

'A ghoul,' Palwahn declared when he returned home, 'a ghoul has no form or shape of its own. Nevertheless it is a most formidable creature. It is as strong as a giant and as disagreeable as an ogre.' He then called on the eccentric widow who had given him the tiny packet containing an egg and a lump of salt. He thanked her and asked for the hand of her daughter.

'But for you, mother,' he told her, 'I should have been a ghoul's food the moment I entered the Valley of Wrath. God be praised, it was a stupid ghoul I came across.'

The Circle round the Throne

BENARES has from time immemorial been famous for its brahmins, bulls, and brocades. Its brahmins are the most orthodox, its bulls the loudest roarers, and its brocades the finest in the world. Yet thanks to the first, the brocademakers were not allowed to own any land in the city of Benares till the time of King Bramha-Datta. 'The brocademakers,' the brahmins used to say, 'are mere weavers: men of low degree. They lack intelligence and scholarship. If they were allowed to settle in the town their stupidity would infect the air. It is best that they should live in the suburbs and ply their craft there—far from the city's heart.'

Now, one day when King Bramha-Datta was sitting on his throne, listening to the petitions of his subjects, the Prime Minister came running to him and whispered, 'Sire! Something terrible has happened. The Mongols have sent us an ambassador extraordinary.'

'Is that so very terrible?' said the King. 'Show him in. We are ready to receive him. There is no reason whatsoever for you to tremble. He is, after all, an ambassador like any other.'

'This Mongol envoy,' the Prime Minister explained, 'is very different from all others. He wants to deliver his message in signs. And that worries me a lot.'

'Well,' the King said, 'if that is the case it can't be helped. Let him deliver his message today, and we shall give our answer tomorrow. That's the best we can do in the circumstances. Surely our wise brahmins will be able to interpret his sign language. It is not polite to keep a foreign envoy waiting. Let him come in.'

At this the Prime Minister went out to usher in the Mongol emissary, and every pair of eyes turned towards the main entrance of the throne room to have the first glimpse of the extraordinary messenger who was going to speak in signs.

The ambassador came in and bowed. He said nothing, but taking a piece of red chalk drew on the floor a large circle with the King's throne as the centre. He then bowed again and withdrew.

'His Excellency will come back tomorrow at this hour for his answer,' said the ambassador's companion and interpreter. And then he too withdrew with a bow.

'It is puzzling,' murmured the King.

'It is indeed so,' echoed the courtiers, while the Prime Minister stroked his chin wondering as much as the others about the red circle round the throne.

Later on, when alone with the Prime Minister, King Bramha-Datta asked, 'What was the message of the Mongol envoy?'

'Sire,' replied the Prime Minister, 'I think he wished to say your throne is the very centre of the earth: your seat is a seat of glory.'

'Nonsense,' said the King and laughed. 'I am not so innocent as to believe that the formidable Mongols have sent their envoy over mountains and deserts to deliver a message of this sort. Maybe, it is a declaration of war. Anyway, what answer are we to give?'

The Prime Minister adjusted his turban, thought for some time as he caressed his chin, and finally declared that he did not know what to say. He had consulted all the learned brahmins and they too were as mystified as he. 'We are not concerned with conundrums,' the brahmins had told him. 'Our job is to interpret the scriptures. Go, and consult the bulls: they may give a reply in signs.' So, the Prime Minister added, he was worried.

'And did you try out the bulls?' the King asked jokingly.

'I did,' the Prime Minister replied. 'But they gave no answer either!'

'I guessed that much. But what about the brocademakers?'

'Sire, they are more stupid than the brahmany bulls.'

'Maybe, you are right,' said the King. 'Maybe, you are not. However, you should do well to consult them. Anyway, we must be ready with our answer tomorrow morning. Other-wise,' he ended, 'you understand . . .' He did not finish his sentence.

The Prime Minister nodded. He understood what the King meant: if there was no answer forthcoming by the next sunrise the Prime Minister would lose his post. Bramha-Datta was a man of his word.

So the harassed Prime Minister hastened to consult the weavers.

But there were no brocademakers to be found anywhere! Being banned from the city they had gradually withdrawn from the suburbs as well. The poor Prime Minister was at his wits' end. He called for the watchmen, and they were instructed to question everyone in Benares and its environments for an answer to the Mongolian envoy's message. And everyone—man, woman, and child—gave a puzzled stare when interrogated. None knew the answer. The enigma of the circle round the throne remained unsolved.

The Prime Minister was on his knees praying hard when a watchman came in to report: 'Perhaps I have found the man who knows the answer.'

'Where?' asked the Prime Minister jumping to his feet. 'Where is he? Bring him here at once.'

'That's not so easy, sir,' the watchman murmured. 'He is a difficult man: the only brocademaker living in the suburbs of Benares. And he refuses to come inside the city unless he is especially invited by the King.'

'The cheek,' muttered the Prime Minister. 'Tell me, what makes you think that this arrogant man knows the answer? He is a weaver, you say. As a rule, the weavers are inscrutably dull. I think he is stupid as well as overbearing. He must be an exceptional idiot.'

'Not this one, sir,' the watchman said. 'On the contrary, he seems to be exceptionally clever. For when I entered his house by the riverside I found there a cradle swinging by itself.'

'That's curious.'

'And that was exactly what I said to myself. Then I thought it would be worthwhile to see the owner. So I pushed open the door leading to the inner hall, and immediately a bell began to ring on its own.'

'What happened next?' asked the Prime Minister.

The watchman recounted that a passage through the inner hall led to the back garden of the brocademaker's cottage, and there was a patch of corn growing by the riverside where a willow swished its branches perpetually to chase away the birds. 'Though mind you,' he added, 'there was no wind. The tree seemed to move its arms by itself. And I repeated to myself, "This is most curious." I then looked round and cried, "Ho! Where's the owner?" "I am in the workshop," someone replied.'

'Make your story short,' said the Prime Minister impatiently. 'Did you talk to him? What did he say?'

'I saw him sitting at his loom, guiding his threads. He did nothing else. He has made a machine which works by the current of the river: it swings his child's cradle, it makes his bell ring, its swishes the arms of his willow, it makes his loom work. "So," I said to myself, "here is my man." And I told him all about the red circle drawn round the throne by the Mongol envoy.'

'A maker of mere mechanical toys!' the Prime Minister sneered. Nevertheless, curiosity prompted him to ask, 'What was his answer?'

'He laughed as he thumped me on the back and said, "Go, and fetch the King before I give the answer." "You want the King and nobody else!" I cried. To this he replied, "The Prime Minister will do, hurry." I have hurried, and here I am.'

'Show me the way,' the Prime Minister said. By now he was convinced that the weaver in question was truly an exceptional man. 'It is already late. There is no time to lose.'

The brocademaker laughed heartily when he heard the Prime

Minister's story, and then told him not to worry as it was not yet morning.

'Do you understand my plight, goodman?' the worried Prime Minister said. 'I am trembling in my shoes. Not so much for myself as for the reputation of Benares. To be baffled by a Mongol envoy! Oh, the shame of it. Please give the correct answer, and you will get anything you ask for. Our King Bramha-Datta is a man of his word.'

'Don't worry, Prime Minister,' the brocademaker repeated. 'Come back tomorrow before sunrise. The answer will be ready then.'

The next morning when the Prime Minister came to fetch the brocademaker he found him arranging a few odd things to put them in a bag: a pair of knucklebones, a toy fiddle, some walnuts, and a small cage containing a pair of tame sparrows.

'What are these for?' asked the surprised Prime Minister.

'For the Mongol envoy,' the brocademaker replied. 'These will certainly undo him.'

A blare of trumpets announced the entry of the Mongol ambassador extraordinary into the throne room of King Bramha-Datta. He came in and bowed as before. This time he took a seat facing the King as his companion and interpreter beckoned for an answer to the enigma of the red circle round the throne.

'On behalf of our gracious sovereign,' the Prime Minister announced, 'our trusted friend, the master brocademaker of Benares will give the answer.'

At this the weaver got up and placed his knucklebones on the floor beside the envoy. The Prime Minister and the courtiers held their breath, wondering if that was the correct answer to the problem posed by the mysterious circle of red chalk. Meanwhile, the Mongol ambassador gave a contemptuous glance at the knucklebones and rose to draw a much smaller circle round the throne in black chalk—or was it a piece of charcoal?—and then returned to his seat.

Every pair of eyes now scrutinised the brocademaker: what was he going to do? He took out his toy fiddle from his bag and started a gay dance tune. To this the Mongol envoy replied by taking out of his pocket a handful of seed grains and scattering them on the floor. The weaver immediately produced his pair of tame sparrows and set them down, and these ate up the grains in less time than it takes to tell.

Now the envoy laid on the floor a piece of chain-mail—one of his epaulettes, and the weaver responded by piercing it with a pair of needles, the finest ones he used for making his brocades. Both the envoy and his companion-interpreter picked up these needles and examined them carefully: they then shook their heads and bowed to each other. Our weaver now came forward with one of his walnuts and gave it to the envoy, who cracked it between his thumb and forefinger as easily as one would crush a fried peanut shell.

A sigh rose from the Prime Minister and the courtiers gasped, for the nut was found to be hollow and filled with dew. They stared hard at the weaver: was he, after all, going to let down the King of Benares by offering a plenipotentiary a bad walnut? But the brocademaker simply beamed. He twirled his thumbs when he saw the envoy and his companion-interpreter turn ashen and hold their breath as the drop of dew rolled out and proved to be a brocaded silk shawl, full ten yards long and ten yards broad.

The Mongol ambassador then rose gravely from his seat for the last time to bid farewell. He bowed, joining his stretched palms to salute in the Indian fashion, and our weaver slipped two walnuts into his cupped hands. The companion-interpreter also saluted in the same way to take his departure; and he too was given a walnut by the weaver.

They then left the court without uttering a word.

When the fanfare for their departure had ended, King Bramha-Datta summoned the weaver to his side and said, 'You have guessed the riddles of the Mongols and answered them correctly. Now ask me what you will, and it will be yours. But pray tell me what all this means. No one in the court has understood a thing.'

'Sire,' answered the brocademaker, 'the meaning is quite simple. The red circle round your throne was the threat, "What will you do if the Mongol forces surround your kingdom?" The answer was: "Knucklebones! What are you compared with us?—Mere children." Toys like knucklebones are the fit things for upstarts.'

'And the meaning of the smaller black circle?'

'It implied, "If the Mongols use the scorched earth policy and came closer to you, what will be your answer?" The response was, "Fiddlesticks!" At this the envoy produced his seed grains to indicate the armies the Mongols can bring into the field. And I replied, "A couple of our tamest, the least equipped armies could annihilate a host of theirs." "Even when protected by chain-mail?" "Yes, even then. And if you don't believe me, Sir envoy, please examine the quality of the steel of my needles." And that, Sire, settled the issue.'

'Then,' asked the King, 'what about the walnuts?'

'Simply to emphasise the message of the needles: "A nation of craftsmen clever enough to make ten square yards of brocade look like a dewdrop can also manufacture weapons capable of piercing through any chain-mail." The other three walnuts were also filled with pieces of Benares silk, and these were gifts for the Mongol ruler. Seeing is believing,' the brocademaker went on, 'and I am sure the Mongol ruler would not believe a word of his envoy's story without some convincing tangible proof. So I gave away a few yards of brocade which any man can easily buy in the bazaars of Benares.'

'Now,' said the King, 'tell me your price. You have saved my honour and brought credit to Benares. What would you like to have for your services?'

The brocademaker did not ask for gold nor for gems, but simply that he and his brother craftsmen should be privileged to have the same rights as the brahmins and bulls in Benares.

And since that day the best brocademakers of India have made Benares their home, and the greatest poet of Benares, Kabir, chose the profession of a weaver to earn his daily bread. 'While,' said he, 'the wisdom of the learned comes from the opportunity of his leisure, the wisdom of the craftsman comes from the perfect mastery of his craft.'

The Four Fortune-seekers

I N VISHNUPUR there were four austere scholars living together as the best of friends. They had studied the science of grammar for twelve consecutive years and spent twelve more in mastering the scriptures; but by the time they had finished their studies and become truly accomplished, they found they were in a bad plight: their legacies were exhausted and not one patron was willing to make them an allowance. So they sat down together to think out what they should do to make a living.

'Vishnupur,' one of them lamented, 'is no place for men like us. Here scholarship is execrated. Look at the people! They spend their time and fortune on cock-fighting, donkey-racing, pig-chasing, elephant-riding, and such silly things. They would never dream of inviting a scholar to expound the abstruser passages of the scriptures or to explain the finer grammatical problems raised in gnomic poetry.'

'And,' sighed the other three, 'they think less of paying him a fee. They are rich enough to burn money on wrestlers imported from abroad; but ask them to spend a cent on a local grammarian and you will hear them groan about their poverty.'

'Yes,' the first scholar continued: 'They will gladly empty out their treasure chests to hire a vulgar dancer, but will grudge us a free meal. Let us leave this place and go elsewhere to seek our furtune.'

'You are right,' replied his friends in unison and quoted the scriptures to justify their point of view.

And the first scholar—not to be outdone in the game of making suitable quotations—cited an illustrative passage from a most ancient and obscure grammar and concluded with some verses:

> Crows and good-for-noughts and deer
> Shrinking from a foreign strand

From their well-trod paths won't veer:
They'd rather perish where they stand.

'Let us clear out of this unlucky place as soon as possible,'
they all said. And having resolved on foreign travel they consulted a wise old woman on the direction they should take in
order to find a fortune.

This woman, though nearly sightless and almost stone deaf,
was reputed to be sagacious: remarkably oracular, uncannily
gifted with the sixth sense, and well versed in the art of magic.
The moment the four scholars crossed her threshold to bow
down at her feet, she murmured:

> 'Mere scholarship is less than sense
> Unless spiced with intelligence.'

They had hardly begun their story when she said, 'Why
don't you try to make your fortune here, in Vishnupur itself?'

'We must, mother,' replied the first scholar, 'leave this place
for good. For Vishnupur is the native city of the crocodiles of
hypocrisy.' 'It is,' the second one added, 'the lair of the serpents
of sin.' 'Furthermore,' the third one remarked, 'it is the tavern
of the mead of the senses.' 'And,' the fourth one exclaimed, 'it
is the slaughterhouse of all goodness.' Then they all pleaded
together, 'Please, mother, help us. Fate has been hard upon us.
Do help us to win a fortune quickly. We are famished.'

'Dear, dear,' the old woman mumbled as she gave them food
and drink. Then she said, 'Believe me, my poor scholars,

> Fortune made in a day,
> Very soon goes away.

As for Fate, you who are learned should know:

> Man's effort (sufficiently great)
> Can equal the wonders of Fate.

But as you are determined to leave Vishnupur for good I am
giving you four magic quills, one for each. Now take the road
to the northern slope of the Himalayas, and wherever a quill
drops of its own accord there its owner will surely find a

treasure. Don't grasp the quills too hard or too lightly, and bear in mind, dear sons, my final warning:

Venture far, but not too far,
Be bold, but not too bold,
Lest like the ignorant beggar
You taste both fire and cold.'

The four scholars did as they were told.

They had not gone far when the leader's quill dropped, and when the spot was examined it was found to be all copper. 'Here's wealth enough for all of us,' he cried. 'What's the use of venturing further?'

'Don't be silly,' said the others. 'A copper mine isn't worth much. Let us go farther and see what happens. We have hardly started on our journey. Perhaps you held your quill lightly. Naturally, it dropped.'

'In that case,' their leader said, 'you may go on; but I will stay here and wait till you come back to fetch me.'

So the three scholars went on. Soon afterwards the second scholar's quill dropped to the ground. And he said, 'Let us stop here. The soil of this spot is, I find, all silver. Take, my friends, as much silver as you will and fetch our poor comrade who is sitting on a heap of paltry copper.'

'You are just as foolish as he!' exclaimed the other two. 'A silver mine cannot be called a real treasure. We must venture farther to find something better.'

'Well,' said the second scholar, 'I am going to stay here.'

The third scholar found in the same way a mine of gold nuggets and there he stopped, while the fourth one went farther on, hugging his quill and saying to himself, 'Surely I shall hit upon a mine of gems. A tiny gem is worth a ton of gold.'

He pressed onward all alone till he reached the regions covered with perpetual snow. There by day it was burning hot and at night it was freezing cold. Going still farther he found on a plateau, covered with solid ice, a man crying in agony as blood dripped down his body: for a toothed iron discus was whirling round his head, sawing through the bones of his skull.

30

It was a most painful sight. The scholar hastened to this man and said, 'What's the meaning, Sir, of the ordeal you are suffering? Is there anything I can do for you? But first tell me if any water can be found here. My tongue is dry: I am dying of thirst.'

At this the man started laughing, while the toothed iron discus left his head to settle on the scholar's. 'Now,' he said mockingly, 'now you know the answer. Once I came here, dear scholar, with a quill in my hand, and found another man in this very plight. And the moment I asked him what he was doing in this God-forsaken place his discus settled on my head. You wait here till another quill-carrying fortune-seeker turns up.'

'But,' the fourth scholar cried, 'my pain is excruciating. I can't bear it long. I am going to die soon.'

'Don't worry,' the other replied. 'You won't die so easily. Whom the gods punish do not die before the appointed hour. Now farewell! On my way home I shall not fail to give your news to your three friends.'

Now these friends of his, having waited for him for a long while, were already on their way to the high plateau of the Himalayas when they met the man lately freed from the torture of the toothed discus. They heard everything from him.

'As you are not carrying any quills,' they were told, 'you cannot be of any service to your friend. Therefore, you would do well to share out the wealth of your mines of copper, silver, and gold. Make the most of your fortune.'

'But,' they stammered, 'we have not marked the sites of the mines. How shall we ever find them again?'

'That's the question! Like me, you did not let the wise old woman of Vishnupur finish her story of the foolish beggar who tasted both fire and cold by venturing too far and being overbold.'

How Princess Maya got her Deserts

THE AGED King Mandhata of Sravasti was a widower, who was proud of his two daughters, Madri and Maya. The princesses were pretty and looked very much alike: for they were twins. Their ways, however, were different.

Madri rarely ventured beyond the palace precincts and gossiped among her companions about the court happenings. But her sister, Maya, usually talked about the delights of travelling and about the pleasures of a scholar's life in far off Benares (where she had finished her studies): a most unusual thing for a princess to do. Among other things Maya had learnt in Benares, thanks to her devotion to a wise ascetic, was the language of animals: something unheard of among the people of Sravasti.

Another thing is worth noticing: while Madri bowed every morning at her father's feet with the greeting, 'Victory, O King! Long live the Monarch of Sravasti!' Maya saluted him with the strange formula: 'Good morning, dear father. Your deserts!'

This sorely irritated the King, and he began getting annoyed with Maya. And one day he lost his temper altogether when a peal of laughter from her woke him from his afternoon slumbers.

'What has happened, young lady?' he demanded angrily. He thought Princess Maya was laughing at him, though this was not the case. 'Cannot a man enjoy his siesta in peace?' he asked. 'Or snore comfortably if he wants to?'

'I did not laugh, father,' Maya replied, 'because you were snoring.'

'What was it then?'

'I overheard the conversation of two ants as they were crawling about your divan.'

'You seem to know a lot of things! Even the language of the ants! Pray, what did the ants say?'

At first Maya was unwilling to reveal what she had unwittingly overheard. But as the King was insistent she said that the two ants were talking about their domestic worries; both of them had grown-up daughters, but no suitable candidates to lead these ant-maidens to the altar. 'One of the ants,' Maya continued, 'said to the other, "Surely, the King will give a magnificent banquet at the wedding of his twin daughters, and all the ants of the land will flock to it. We shall then easily find from among them suitable grooms for our girls." The other replied, "Well, let us hope so. But what beats me is the King's coolness. How can he snore in peace when he has two grown-up unmarried daughters under his roof?" This,' Maya added, 'made me laugh.'

'Hum, hum,' muttered the King as he turned round on his divan pretending to be too sleepy to follow Maya's account any further. 'Hum,' he repeated with his eyes closed. But sleep had left him for good.

The next morning after receiving the usual greetings from his two daughters, the King called for his Chief Counsellor and told him, 'There is something definitely wrong with Princess Maya. She speaks malevolently. She deserves to be punished.'

'Love,' said the Chief Counsellor to himself, 'love when it turns sour, turns very sour indeed.'

'Now,' the King went on, 'let me know what you think. It's no use staring at me as though you were deaf.'

'The subject,' the Chief Counsellor stammered, 'is rather delicate.'

'So, what about it? Are you not my principal adviser, the Chief Counsellor of State? If I can't talk over such things with you, whom am I to consult? What am I to do?'

'If the Queen were alive she could have explained the matter to you.'

'But,' the King interrupted, 'she is dead. She died twenty years ago, when these girls were born.'

'That's it. There you have the answer, sire. Your daughters are no longer mere girls. They are in early womanhood. It's time for them to get married.'

'Married!' the King groaned. 'Easier said than done! Where am I to find husbands for them?'

The Chief Counsellor murmured something about the professional matchmakers who had lists of suitable candidates at their finger-tips.

'Hum,' said the King and heaved a deep sigh. 'No one is likely to accept any of them without a handsome dowry. And my treasury is empty.'

At this the Chief Counsellor mumbled about the poor and how their daughters got their husbands; but he did not get the chance of finishing what he had to say. For the King began almost immediately, 'Tell me, my all-knowing Counsellor, why does Maya behave differently from her sister Madri? Both were born under the same star, at the same time, and both look very much the same. In fact they are as alike as two peas in the same pod.'

'Perhaps their minds are different: just as their finger-prints are different. I think Princess Maya badly needs a husband.' And as the King did not interrupt him this time the Chief Counsellor expounded at length his view, which in brief was simply this: 'It is better for an intelligent young lady like Princess Maya to have a difficult or a poor husband than to have no husband at all.'

'Hum, hum,' said the King as he dismissed the Chief Counsellor to think over things by himself.

However, the more he thought the more he felt that Princess Maya was malevolent and so she deserved to be punished. He could not rid himself of the idea. Therefore the following morning when the princesses came to greet him in their usual way, he stopped Maya and told her, 'Young lady, you will have your own deserts today. I have made up my mind, and you will be given in marriage to a stranger at sundown. Have you anything to say?'

Princess Maya was too astonished at this sudden decision of the King to utter a single word.

'There is,' the King continued, 'a newcomer in our temple yard: a most greedy mendicant hailing from Avanti. He is the first person I saw this morning when I looked out of my window. He will be your husband, and you will have to leave my kingdom with him soon after your wedding.'

So as her punishment Princess Maya was given in marriage to an exceptionally lean beggar who had made the Devi temple of Sravasti his temporary shelter. She brought no dowry with her: only such ornaments as she had on her person were her marriage portion. The giving away of the bride was done by the Chief Counsellor.

The King was too angry with Maya to witness—and, still less, to participate in—the wedding ceremony. However, a couple of days later, when somewhat calmed, he asked the Chief Counsellor, 'Did that beggar from Avanti expect a huge dowry?'

'No, sire.'

'Didn't he know that I wanted to punish Maya? Did he say anything?'

'Yes, sire. "I have received my deserts," he said, "and I am thankful. Now I shall travel happily with my wife." He has, in fact, already left Sravasti with Princess Maya.'

'Now,' Princess Madri broke in, 'what did my sister say? Was she very unhappy?'

'Judging from her looks,' the Chief Counsellor replied, 'one would say she was delighted.'

'Maya pretended to be happy,' the King interrupted, 'out of sheer malevolence. But did she not give any parting message to Madri? A note of warning, or some such thing?'

The Chief Counsellor murmured that Princess Maya's parting remarks were hardly worth repeating, especially as she was now on her way to a strange country. However, when pressed hard he declared that Maya believed that it would do Madri good to bear in mind the saying:

Better to have a beggar as spouse
Than dwell alone in a great king's house.

'This is a conundrum,' he added immediately. 'A popular saying, a mere word-play. One mustn't pay any heed to it.'

'It is a silly saying, I agree,' Princess Madri remarked. 'Maya's studies at Benares must have turned her head.'

'That is the case,' the King added. 'Let us see how her learning helps her to get along in life.'

Now the beggar who took Princess Maya as wife was no beggar at all. He was not really a vagrant nor a mendicant though he was continually moving about from one shrine to another. He did this, he confessed to Maya, because he was thoroughly ashamed of himself.

'Ashamed!' said Maya, interrupting her husband. 'Ashamed of what?'

There was a lump in the poor man's throat and it grew larger every moment. Maya being understanding by nature came closer to him and clasped his hands to give him assurance. She then said, 'Just whisper in my ear and let me share your burden. Tell me, what makes you feel ashamed of yourself?'

'I am ashamed of my incurable greediness,' he replied. 'No doctor can cure me. I have the stomach of a wolf. I gorge enough for ten, yet my body wastes daily in every limb.'

'What sort of a doctor did you consult? Is he a good man?'

'Well, my dear bride, I did not consult just one doctor, but very many. My father invited every physician of renown to Avanti to examine me; but not one of them found a cure.'

'Then what happened?' asked Maya. 'What made you leave home?'

One day, he explained, a most famous doctor after pocketing his fee—a heavy fee—propounded the view that he was perhaps a changeling—a beggar's son—and therefore was for ever eating voraciously and profiting little from what he partook. 'The only cure,' he went on, 'according to this doctor, was to make

36

a clean breast of it and to expose myself in beggar's rags. So I ran away from home.'

'Did your parents ask you to leave their house?'

'No,' he replied. 'They did not. On the contrary, they turned the doctor out without letting him finish his exposition. But I ran away secretly on my own. And the best I could do was to wander from one temple to another leading a beggar's life and hoping this would cure my disease.'

'Don't worry,' Maya said when she had heard all that her husband had to say. 'Don't worry,' she repeated. 'I shall find a cure for you. Just give me a few days to think things over.'

Maya drew her own conclusions from what she was told, and reasoned in this way: her husband could not be a change-ling, for were he so he would have been voracious from his babyhood. And this was not the case. His troubles started, she understood, from the day when he as a young man was found sleeping near a big ant-hill in the forest where he had gone with his retinue to hunt. 'My father-in-law,' she mused, 'must be a man of means. Otherwise he could not have sent my husband out hunting with a number of retainers. And then how could he afford to invite doctors from all over the country to Avanti were he not wealthy? Now my husband is trying to hide his identity from me lest I insist on his returning home before he has been cured. Very well, I shall rid him of his voracity, and then see what happens.'

When in the course of their wanderings they came near a huge ant-hill by the edge of a lake, Maya decided to stop there for a while. 'My husband's troubles started,' she said to herself, 'when he was found asleep near such an ant-hill. Maybe, the present one will give me some clue.' So she said to him, 'Dear heart, let us repose here under the mango trees. The view from this spot is simply wonderful. As you look tired I ought to get some food for you. There is a town nearby, and I shall see what can be bought there.'

'Don't you want me to accompany you?' asked her husband.

'I should love it. But you do look exhausted. And then it is better for a woman to be alone when she wants to sell or pawn a bracelet. You just lie down here in the shade and have a short nap, if you will. Meanwhile, I shall run to the town and buy all we need by getting rid of one of my bracelets.'

'Then do hurry. I shall wait for you here under the mango trees.'

'I shan't take long,' said Maya as she hastened to the town to do her shopping.

When her shopping was done Princess Maya returned to the spot where she had left her husband. She found him fast asleep with his face turned towards the ant-hill. And she noticed issuing from his mouth the head of a hooded snake, taking air. At first the reptile was thin as a thread, but gradually it grew in girth till it became a huge cobra. She saw also another cobra crawling out of the ant-hill, apparently for the same purpose, to take the air.

She gasped in amazement and stood still, hiding herself behind a tree trunk. As she understood the language of animals, she naturally pricked up her ears to listen to the conversation of the two snakes.

Now these two hooded serpents approached each other with eyes reddened with rage. 'You rascal!' hissed the ant-hill cobra. 'You rascal! How dare you torment a handsome young prince and reduce him to beggary, changing him to a mere bag of bones? You are meaner than a worm. Even an eyeless slug finds its own food, but you are too lazy to do that. You eat up whatever is put into the prince's mouth, and if this goes on any longer he will die of sheer starvation. You are vile.'

'You are vile yourself!' the other snake hissed back. 'You are a low beast. How can you shamelessly bemire the priceless treasure-trove lying under that ant-hill? What good are you doing to yourself or to anyone else by befouling every day the richest hoard of jewels in the world? You can't eat them. Can you? You are simply jealous of me!'

38

'Jealous of a vile creature like you! Tell me another. What a pity no one has thought of putting a handful of black mustard seed into the prince's mouth and killing you outright in this simple way.'

'And,' the other cobra retorted, 'the easiest way of getting rid of a pest like you would be to drench the ant-hill with a bucket of hot vinegar!'

Now you may well guess what happened next. Maya overheard all this conversation, and she did just as the two snakes had suggested for killing each other. Thus she cured her husband with a handful of black mustard seed and secured for herself—with the help of a bucket of hot vinegar—a priceless treasure-trove, dowry enough for any princess in the world.

It turned out that her husband was the Crown Prince of Avanti, and now that he was cured of his voracity he hastened back home with his pretty bride. And there the two were received with great rejoicing and high honours.

Thus Princess Maya got her deserts. She will be long remembered; for she is the author of the popular saying:

> *Be quick with your intelligence*
> *In honest give and take;*
> *Or perish like the ant-hill beast*
> *And like the belly-snake.*

The Munificent Miser

THERE was a merchant in Rajgirh, called Mahajani, who advocated total abstinence. 'Never in my life,' he swore, 'will I taste even a drop of drink.' Not that he had any religious or aesthetic scruples against the flowing bowl, but the plain fact is simply this: though fabulously rich he was grossly niggardly. 'If I drink,' he argued to himself, 'others may want to drink with me, and that would mean ruinous expense.' The very thought of 'others' made the miser's heart sink. For he was a guild-master, and naturally his friends and associates were many. 'To stand a round of drinks to all of them,' he mumbled to himself, 'would bring me disaster.'

Mahajani's father, a large-hearted Good Samaritan, left him an immense fortune. Thanks to this legacy and the respect people bore a generous man's memory, Mahajani came to be elected a guild-master shortly after his father's death. His wife then told him, 'A guild-master, my dear, ought to do some entertaining. We should invite from time to time the members of your guild and their wives and some other people as well.'

'Over my dead body,' Mahajani replied coldly. 'As long as I am alive and kicking you must not dream of entertaining a single soul. Merry-making is money-burning. And I don't like that.'

His wife protested and reminded him that he was quite different when his father was alive. 'You then enjoyed parties,' she said.

'When will you get some sense into your silly little head?' he sniggered. 'In those days I had to pretend that I liked everything our Old Man did. I kept quiet. Otherwise—who knows? —he might have left the bulk of his fortune to the city or to the guild. But, between ourselves, I never relished his burning money on feasts and fairings and other nonsenses.'

Mahajani's wife remained silent. What else could she do?

She admired her father-in-law for his many virtues and, above all, for his hearty generosity and lavish hospitality. She was sorely distressed to hear her husband talk in this way.

As time went on Mahajani's stinginess increased. One day he told his wife emphatically that in future his puddings must be made without raisins.

'What's wrong with raisins?' the surprised wife asked.

'Wine is made from grapes,' he replied. 'And what are raisins? They are sun-dried grapes. I know of people who took to grapejuice extracts and then went to the dogs by becoming too friendly with wine-bibbers. Now, it is no use arguing with me. I simply don't care for raisins. Moreover, they cost a lot of money.'

A few days later he declared that dates were worse than dangerous drugs, for date-liquor was responsible for the ruin of many a decent trader. 'By making them,' he added, 'foolish and extravagant. Such people waste their time and substance in the company of topers. I simply hate the sight of dates. Moreover, they cost a lot of money.'

In this way he found something new every day that had to be removed from the household menu. Finally, he began grudging his wife the money for housekeeping and suppressed her pin-money altogether. The poor woman thought he was going off his head. So she pawned some of her jewellery to consult the most renowned specialists of mental disorders about her husband's parsimony.

'He was not at all like that,' she sobbed, 'when we were first married. He was then like his father, gay and generous. He used to buy me presents every other day and always helped the needy with all his heart. But now he has changed completely. He does not laugh any more and has stopped giving me any money. What has gone wrong with him?' she asked. 'For whom is he working himself to death? We have no children. We are just two in the world, husband and wife.'

The specialists then questioned her closely. And she revealed, rather reluctantly, that Mahajani had broken the tradition of his house by closing down the ancient almonries founded by his forebears and driving the poor—even the religious mendicants and the yellow-robed friars—with blows from his gates. 'Fancy that,' she continued, 'in a house where no one was allowed to go away empty handed! All that interests him now is gold and nothing but gold. One day he may even sell the household furniture and the house itself for gold bars. Why does he desire to hoard so much gold?'

The specialists asked her a few more questions and then after a long confabulation among themselves declared: 'He has been bitten by the gold bug. We have no medicine for him. You may, if you like, appeal to the King.'

'That is out of the question,' she murmured, drying her eyes. 'I don't want a public scandal.'

Now, as far as his routine work was concerned Mahajani carried on with it as efficiently as before; he did not show the least sign of eccentricity. Only his closest business associates noticed certain changes: apart from his miserliness, he was becoming more and more ruthless in driving bargains and his hours of work were increasing steadily.

One day something unusual happened to Mahajani as he was returning home from attendance on the King, then residing in the Summer Palace outside Rajgirh. He noticed a country bumpkin squatting on a bench near a tumble-down tavern, laughing and singing to himself:

'Drinking when I have a mind to,
Singing as I feel inclined to.'

'The foolish fellow!' Mahajani said to himself. 'From his looks he appears to be desperately poor, one living from hand to mouth. Yet he is indulging in the luxury of laughing light-heartedly and singing noisily. Surely he is no ordinary man. Has he perhaps a hidden hoard of gold, a stock much bigger than mine? How,' he went on wondering and arguing to himself, 'how has this man made his pile? Will he reveal his secret to me?' Mahajani sighed wistfully and stopped to watch the antics of the gay yokel.

This man must have journeyed far. For he was covered with dust from head to foot. His clothes were mere rags. There were osier baskets by his side as well as a bamboo carrying-pole. To all appearances he was nothing but a country porter enjoying a brief respite by the roadside, filling a mug from a jar of foul-smelling toddy and drinking it off with a morsel of stinking dried fish as a relish.

'Maybe,' Mahajani mused as his imagination ran wild, 'maybe, this is Kuvera himself, the God of Wealth, in disguise. The ways of the deity, they say, are mysterious. He turns up at un-expected places in strange forms to help the deserving. Appear-ances are generally misleading. The wealthiest Jain I know goes about shoeless, clad in a loin-cloth only. And this man may look like a common load-carrier, but I am sure he isn't one. Otherwise he would not be singing so gaily.' He then approach-ed the arrack-quaffer with deference and bowed reverentially.

At this the country porter signed Mahajani to sit by his side and share his drink with him. Our guild-master hesitated, and his reluctance made the toper bawl:

'Holla ho! Holla ho!
Here's a morose fellow!'

This groggy outburst was interpreted by the miser Mahajani as a hint of the god Kuvera's willingness to help him. So after bowing again he asked of the porter if there was anything better than gold in this world.

'Home brew,' was the porter's answer. 'After home brew comes gold.'

'But where's gold to be found?'

'Why, right here,' the drunken man replied as he stretched himself on his bench and yawned noisily. Before falling into a stupor he muttered something about the joy of living in the country, and about cities being curses where one easily lost one's way. 'And,' he concluded, 'city-dwellers are close-fisted rascals.'

On his return home Mahajani was greeted by his wife. 'What has happened to you, my dear?' she asked anxiously. 'Why are you so late? You look as yellow as old cotton. Are you not feeling well?'

Mahajani refused to give any candid answer, only mumbled about his being unhappy, and begged to be left alone. He then retired to his chamber, and there he lay down, hugging his bed and moaning.

'What's wrong with you?' his wife kept on asking. She simply refused to leave him to himself. 'Do you want me to rub your back? Has that nasty rheumatism come back again?'

'Please,' Mahajani snivelled, 'Dear Wife, get me some home brew. It will, I know, cure me.'

This demand for home brew staggered her. At first she could hardly believe her ears. However, as Mahajani kept on repeating his request she burst into tears: there was hardly any money for food in the household and here was her husband insisting on home brew from a strange tavern! What was she to do?

'The advice of the god Kuvera,' Mahajani kept on, 'must be obeyed. Here is a piece of gold, and please do what I tell you. The matter is most serious. For heaven's sake, do not waste any time.'

The more Mahajani wanted his wife to hurry the more she tarried, wondering what made him think all of a sudden that home brew was a cure for rheumatism. The exasperated guildmaster then told her again that he had been counselled by the oracle of the God of Wealth to drink a jar of spirits near a tumble-down inn outside Rajgirh. And as he did not dare enter the tavern lest he be recognised and forced to stand a round of drinks, she was to go and get a pot of liquor for him and place it near a bench under some acacias.

'If you care for your husband you should hurry,' Mahajani enjoined. 'Please hide the jar in a thicket under the acacias. You can't miss the tumble-down hovel. It is quite a landmark.' He did not give her the chance of asking any further questions as he hustled her out of the house. 'If you don't hurry,' he said as

44

he saw her off, 'Kuvera may reveal his secret to someone else, and the hidden hoard of gold will be gone. I am sure the moment I empty the pot of toddy with some dried fish the deity himself will lead my steps to a secret treasure-trove. Now don't lose any time talking to that chatterbox, our neighbour's wife. By the way, keep the change, if you will, to buy some finery for yourself.'

'It is sheer madness,' Mahajani's wife said to herself, but she did as she was told.

And Mahajani, after emptying the jar of powerful arrack, went straight to the Summer Palace. As he was a well-known guild-master his coming was immediately announced to the King, who received him kindly and said, 'What brings you back at this unusual hour, Lord Guild-Master?'

'I am back, sire,' Mahajani replied, 'because I am worried. I cannot sleep in peace: for I have a million in gold bars in my town house. I should like to place this gold at your disposal. The sooner this is done the better. Therefore deign to have my accumulated store transferred immediately to the royal treasury.'

'No, my lord,' said the King. Reasons of State did not permit this sort of transfer to the king's treasury. The offer was declined with thanks. Mahajani should, it was suggested, distribute his million as he thought fit, without being influenced by the King's likes and dislikes. As Mahajani's father had been renowned for his discretion and discernment in making his charities, he too should do the same. 'I do, all the same,' the King ended, 'appreciate your gesture and thank you very much.'

'As it pleases your majesty,' Mahajani finally said as he withdrew from the King's presence. 'I have made up my mind: I shall give away a million to the needy. Town-criers will proclaim it to all.'

On returning home Mahajani summoned his guards, gatekeepers, gardeners, retainers and servants, and issued orders that if any one resembling him should turn up and claim to be the master of the house they should cudgel that artful impostor and throw him out without ceremony. 'You may,' he added, 'find it difficult to believe. But the fact is, let me assure you, this pretender is as cunning as a fox. He has been following me about like a devoted disciple and has managed to copy my looks and my gestures as well. Don't be taken in by this rogue.'

'Who can this man be?' they all asked, uneasily wondering.

'He must be an out-of-work actor. I espied him in the mirrors of the king's Summer Palace. He was standing behind me like my own shadow. But the moment I turned round to have a good look at him he vanished. He hid himself craftily behind the double-pillars of the hall.'

He then mounted the stairs to the upper story and there greeted his wife with a beaming smile. 'My dear,' he said, 'I don't look yellow any more. Do I? Now let me tell you, I have been to the Summer Palace and have come back with a piece of sound advice: the best means of curing jaundice is to be bountiful. What do you say to this?'

'By all means,' she told him, 'be as charitable as you wish. Certainly you can afford to give away some of your gold. You are the wealthiest guild-master of Rajgirh.'

'It is good to hear that you share my views,' Mahajani said. 'But I am going to our country villa for a while, disguised as a common porter, and you will have to look after the distribution of gifts to the needy. Now don't be peeved about my burying myself in the country for a short time. For,' he emphasised, 'it is the command of the god Kuvera and it cannot be disregarded. Between ourselves, it will not be for the first time that you will be staying here all by yourself.'

His wife assented to this whim of his and promised to distribute gifts to the needy during his absence.

'Send then for the criers,' Mahajani ordered his men. 'Let it be announced with beat of drum through all Rajgirh that any one in need of anything should come to my house and collect what he wants. Meanwhile I shall stay away from here for a few days.'

46

In due course a large crowd flocked to Mahajani's house. The bags and the vessels they brought with them were filled to overflowing with gifts under the supervision of Mahajani's kind-hearted wife.

Among those who sought bounty was one of Mahajani's tenants, a crofter who lived in a corner of the grounds of Mahajani's country villa. He asked for a pair of bullocks and a cart, and not only got what he wanted but also—to his surprise—had the cart loaded with sacks of food grains and seeds. He felt overwhelmed by his master's generosity. On his return home he kept on repeating loudly to himself, 'May you live to be a hundred, my good lord Mahajani! Thanks to your charity I shall pass the rest of my days in perfect happiness. Whose were these fine bullocks ?—Yours. And whose was this splendid cart ? —Yours again. It was no father or mother who gave me these sacks; no, my riches come solely from you, my lord Mahajani.'

Now these words reached Mahajani's ears as he was wandering about the grounds of his villa trying to rid himself of the terrible headache the pot of strong toddy had given him. 'Why,' he said to himself, 'the fellow is mentioning my name in his talk!' He then vaguely recollected that he had called on the King when he was drunk and offered his royal master a million in gold bars. 'Can the King have been distributing my wealth to the people?' he asked himself, and ran to the crofter for an explanation.

'An explanation!' exclaimed the man in indignation. 'Who are you to demand an explanation? Get out of my way, you soaker. Don't try to fool me by calling yourself Mahajani the Guild-Master. I know all about you. Why, all Rajgirh knows about your buffoonery. You may be as clever as a fox, but you are not going to diddle me.'

'Who do you think I am if not the Guild-Master?' asked Mahajani.

'Repeat that in the King's court and be clapped in gaol! I know you are a clever actor, out of work just now. All the same, you are an impostor.' Shaking his fist at Mahajani he continued, 'An artful impostor! You have been shadowing my master and have learnt to imitate his looks and gestures and even his voice. Now, get out of my way.'

Mahajani, however, refused to move. Recognising his own bullocks and cart, he seized the animals by the cord, crying, 'Stop fellow! These are my best bullocks, and the cart is mine.'

At this the crofter gave him a sound drubbing, shouting all the while that he was not going to be cheated by a jobless mummer, a mountebank. And finally taking Mahajani by the throat he flung him back by the way he had come.

Sobered by this rough handling Mahajani limped back to his town house, and there seeing people coming out of the gates laden with his goods, he fell to laying hands on here a man and there another, crying all the while, 'Hi! What's this? It's robbery in broad daylight!' And every man he laid hands on knocked him down, calling him, 'A cheat! A rogue! And an impostor!'

At last bruised and mud-bespattered he tried to seek refuge in his own house when he was stopped by the gate-keepers with, 'Hi! You! Where are you going?'

'To my room,' he said.

'Look at the actor's cheek,' they said to each other. 'He is trying to sneak into our master's chamber!' Without more-a-do they threw him out of doors, showering curses.

Mahajani then hobbled to the Summer Palace. And there he cried as he bowed before the King, 'Why, O why, sire, have you ordered my ruin? Why have you decided to plunder me? All Rajgirh has flocked to my house.'

'No, my Lord Guild-Master,' the King replied. 'It is not I but you yourself who decided to give a million away. Did you not propose that if I refused to accept your gold you would send criers round asking all and sundry to come to your house and take away whatever they wanted?'

Mahajani became confused. He tried to recollect the events

of the day when he had come across a toper outside a tumble-down tavern. He then babbled about someone resembling him, and this man—his double—had probably turned up at the palace! 'Sire,' he said finally, 'surely you know I am extremely frugal. It has never been my custom to give anything away or to waste the least particle of my substance. Is it possible for a man like me to be extravagant? To throw away a million on idlers and good-for-noughts is drunken folly. My double, I am sure, must have misled you and others. I never ordered anything to be given away.'

'Are you sure,' the King now asked, 'you are Mahajani the Guild-Master and not his double?' His suspicion was aroused and he ordered that Mahajani should be detained and his wife invited to identify him.

The poor guild-master began to tremble. He looked at his image in the mirrors adorning the royal court, and was shocked at his own appearance: he could hardly recognise his own self. His hair was dishevelled, his eyes red and swollen, his body covered with mire, and his clothes were mere rags. 'If mother were alive,' he said to himself, 'she would not have recognised me in my present state!' What would happen, he wondered, if his wife declared that he was not himself but his double. What would then become of his immense fortune? Was it then going to be squandered on the lazy beggars of Rajgirh and the countryside? Was there any means of saving the larger portion of his wealth by sacrificing a mere million kept in the vaults of his town house?—These thoughts tormented him and such was his anguish that he fell into a swoon.

When he recovered his senses he found his wife whispering to him, 'Say "yes" to whatever I tell the King, and promise that you will never touch toddy any more.' Mahajani readily acquiesced.

And she, a woman of ready wit, told the King that the mud-bespattered man before her was no other than Mahajani the Guild-Master, her lawful husband—a man of most generous disposition, always inclined to help the needy and patronise all the worthwhile undertakings in the city of Rajgirh. 'Only,' she continued with a feigned sigh of guilt, 'I am a temperamental woman. My vagaries have distracted my husband beyond endurance. He wants to give—in fact, he has always wished to give away half of his earnings. But being economical I have hitherto held back his generous hand. It was I who proposed to him as a joke that he should spread the story of his double. But now,' she kept on with downcast eyes, 'I repent my folly. Let it be known in future that my husband keeps an open house, and I as mistress of his hearth shall gladly offer hospitality to all callers and bestow charity on all who are needy. My husband is wealthy enough to give away a million. With the blessing of Kuvera and under your protection, Sire,' she ended, 'may we have the joy of giving away much more. We are but two in this world—husband and wife—and what can we do with our wealth except share it with others?'

Mahajani nodded his assent to everything his wife said.

'Mistress,' the King declared, 'it is good of you to make this public confession. You have earned our thanks. And as for your husband, in future he shall be known as Mahajani the Munificent.'

And that was what really happened: the erstwhile miser became truly munificent. In the course of time both he and his wife came to believe that it was Kuvera, the God of Wealth—and not a common country porter—who changed their way of living, and made them the most loved couple of all Rajgirh. Perhaps they were not wrong in their surmise.

The End of the World

THE ELDER of the village of Falguni enjoyed his midday siesta more than his sleep at night. He was therefore in no mood for jokes, to put it mildly, when the Watchman roused him with his cry of alarm.

'What has happened?' asked the old man gruffly, opening only one eye. 'Is the house on fire?'

'No, sir,' the Watchman said. 'Something worse, much worse. Something dreadful.'

'Dreadful?'

'More dreadful than fire, flood, or famine.'

This made the Elder sit up and open both his eyes. He then grasped at his staff, which was by his side. By now he was wide awake. What was an Elder, in spite of his flowing beard, without his massive staff? He knew, a king without his crown was no king, and a man of his rank without his insignia of office was a simple nobody in an emergency: the staff was his insignia. 'Eh, what is it?' the Elder asked as he caressed his staff.

'Something more terrible than the triple disaster,' repeated the trembling Watchman.

And what could that be? The Elder looked out of the window. Outside the sky was deep blue. The sun was shining as usual, and the cicadas were singing noisily in their accustomed way. There was nothing strange as far as he could judge in the glare and the heat. He blew his nose and sniffed the air: it gave no indication of a burning smell. So there was no fear of a big fire. As for flood, that was out of the question in a land known for its dearth of water. Famine was equally unthinkable. 'Tell me,' the Elder finally repeated, 'what is it?'

'Sir, the end of the world is at hand.'

'But,' said the Elder hitting the floor hard with his staff, 'I have not heard the sound of the trumpet.'

'The brayings of the asses have proclaimed it.'

The Elder was God-fearing, but short tempered. He swore horribly and declared that of all blasphemies it was the worst blasphemy to aver that the Rider of the White Horse of the Judgment Day would choose a donkey for his mount: it was contrary to everything in the scriptures. 'You are an ass,' he exclaimed thumping again his staff on the ground. 'Have the asses talked to you?'

'Yes, sir,' the Watchman answered. 'They have.'

'And I presume you are the only one to whom the asses have spoken.'

The Watchman shook his head vigorously: he was not the only one to hear the asses speak. There was the Inn-keeper who could attest the fact. 'He is already on his way,' he added. 'He will be here as soon as he has given the sheep some water to drink.'

'The Inn-keeper is an ass himself,' the Elder muttered. 'You two have been drinking. That's the long and short of the matter.'

The Watchman protested: first he rarely drank except on festive occasions; and then, never in the middle of the day.

'All right,' said the Elder. 'Bring the talking asses to me. I want to hear them speak.'

'But they have run away.'

'Where to? To whom do they belong?'

'How do I know, sir?' The Watchman shrugged his shoulders. 'As soon as they were given a drink of water,' he continued, 'they changed into men. "Let us escape," they then said to one another, "before the terrible magician returns." And without a word more they fled. Neither the Inn-keeper nor I could do anything about it. To tell you the truth, it took my breath away to see a donkey become a man. One was bad enough. But before my very eyes one after another, the twelve of them became men. God! How I trembled and was altogether tongue-tied.'

'It was the same with me,' interrupted the Inn-keeper, who had come in while the Watchman was explaining the meta-morphosis of a string of twelve donkeys. 'I could hardly believe my eyes,' he went on. 'Never have I seen such a thing before. The sight changed my blood into water. I could not help it any more than my friend the Watchman. However, he is luckier. He did not stay to see the sheep changed into boys. I think, sir,' he finally declared, 'the end of the world is at hand. What are we to do?'

After further questioning the Elder fell in a state of abstraction as if he had fallen asleep with his eyes wide open. The news was ominous, in effect stupefying. He could judge for himself that the two men standing before him were telling the truth. He ransacked his memory to recall a single instance of such a happening. As a boy he had heard of a troublesome woman changed into a crow: it was, however, a mere story current among a group of nonagenarian gossipmongers; one could not possibly cite it in a court of law. And then that was the case of a human being degraded into a feathered creature, whereas the present incident was very different: lower animals transformed into men and boys. What ought to be done about it?

A few days earlier when the Watchman and the Inn-keeper were having a quiet game of chess a saffron-robed man carrying a trident in his hand stopped before them and asked, 'Are the stables in this inn any good?'

The Inn-keeper did not bother to look up, for he felt offended. The saffron-robed stranger was staying, he knew, in a derelict monastery outside Falguni instead of stopping in his well-appointed guest-house. This monastery was in ruins, and no one lived there. Its once famous lily pool was now over-grown with weeds; and its water, turned into a smoky green colour, issued an awful stench. 'A man living in that filthy foxhole,' the Inn-keeper murmured to himself, 'has no business to bother about the condition of my stables. And then where are his horses? Let the animals lodge with their master!'

'I say,' said the stranger clanging the rings attached to the handle of his trident, 'I say, are the stables here big enough for a score of animals?'

'Of course,' replied the Watchman, 'they are. Men who go to the horse fair at Tamluk stop here.'

'But where are your horses?' asked the Inn-keeper without deigning to raise his head.

'Not horses,' said the saffron-robed stranger. 'But donkeys and sheep. About twenty in all. I shall bring them in batches. Can you lodge them for about a week?'

'Of course, that can be done,' answered the Inn-keeper, and then after some bargaining came to terms with the newcomer about the charges.

The Watchman now wanted to know where the man came from and where he was going. To this the answer was: 'I am from Kamrup. And as soon as I have collected my animals I shall go back there.' Finally, turning to the Inn-keeper, the stranger said, 'My animals do not need any water. Please don't give them any.'

The saffron-robed stranger from Kamrup brought his animals, as he had said, in small batches. They looked no different from ordinary donkeys and common sheep, only they were exceptionally quiet. And no one would have known they were men and boys turned into animals had they not been offered water one day when it was exceptionally hot.

It was the Watchman who had proposed that the animals should be given a good drink of water. 'For,' he told the Inn-keeper, 'Kamrup is a long way off. As your man is going away early tomorrow morning it will be better to give these poor creatures their fill of water now. They have all started braying and bleating piteously.'

'Perhaps you are right,' said the Inn-keeper. 'The man of Kamrup is surely an eccentric. Maybe, he believes all water here to be as foul as that of the stinking pond of the tumble-down monastery.'

So the two friends stopped their usual game of chess and filled to the brim the water troughs inside the stables. And then the curious miracle happened: the moment the donkeys and the sheep had their first quaff they rolled on the ground braying and bleating, and a second later changed into men and boys. Then they all ran out of the stables and fled from Falguni as fast as their legs could carry them.

'What are we to do now?' the surprised Watchman asked his equally astonished friend, the Inn-keeper.

'Run to the Elder! This is black magic. The end of the world is at hand.'

'So that's that,' said the Elder after he had grasped the details of the affair. 'Now what's to be done about it? I agree with you: this is purely black art. We must proceed carefully.'

'The man of Kamrup is coming back later this afternoon,' the Inn-keeper said, 'to settle his bills. He will leave Falguni tomorrow at dawn.'

'Tell him, when he comes,' the Elder advised, 'the animals have been well looked after. And as you have played host to them all these days he in his turn ought to play host to you and to your friend the Watchman. Then see what happens. If he does not agree, bring him over to me. Perhaps,' he added, 'we ought to give him something to drink to make him jovial.'

The Inn-keeper followed the Elder's advice, and he as well as the Watchman were cordially invited by the man of Kamrup to dinner in the monastery that evening.

The two friends went together at the appointed hour, expecting, however, that nothing would be ready for them. On their way the Watchman remarked, 'I am sure our saffron-robed man has vanished.'

'Perhaps, he has,' the Inn-keeper said. 'Between ourselves, I have got over my fright about this man.'

'So have I. Only an hour ago I heard that conjurors at Tamluk show all sorts of tricks. Someone told me that he has seen a woman sawn in half and then made whole again. He saw this in Benares.'

'And then,' said the Inn-keeper, 'when I come to think of it, the mango trick they show in our own fairs is no less astonishing. You know, they thrust a magic stone in the ground and before your own eyes a plant immediately sprouts, and in a few minutes grows into a tree of a man's height and then becomes bigger while its branches bear ripe mangoes which the conjuror gives people to eat. Now,' he concluded, 'that is as good as changing a man into a donkey or a donkey into a man.'

'It will be amusing to see what our saffron-robed magician gives us to eat tonight. That ruined monastery has not even a proper kitchen.'

'It never had one for a long time, as far as I can recall. It has been derelict for ages.'

However, to their great astonishment they found, as soon as they had gone through the front gate, that the courtyard of the monastery had recently been repaired handsomely. The place was delightfully illuminated with coloured lanterns. Its pond was a pleasure to the eye, brimming with crystal clear water bearing blue nenuphars and golden lotuses whose delicate perfume pervaded the whole atmosphere. The refectory to which they were led by the man of Kamrup was richly decorated and lit with graceful candelabras and crystal chandeliers. It was magnificently furnished, more luxuriously appointed than the banqueting hall of a king.

'Don't be surprised,' the host said to his two guests. 'The repairs have been done secretly. Of course, the inmates of the monastery are not as numerous as they used to be a thousand years ago when our order was first founded. The world has changed a lot. By the way,' he spoke in an apologetic tone, 'we are Tantriks, and our order does not believe in austerity. On the contrary, we think it is sinful to punish the flesh.'

The food was served on silver platters by a number of boys, all about sixteen years of age; they were dressed in the robes belonging to novices of a long extinct Tantrik order. The dishes were exquisite; the fruits were the most delicious the two men of Falguni had ever tasted.

'I have a surprise for you,' the host whispered when the dinner was over. 'Though this is not done in other monasteries,

I have arranged for some profane music. You don't mind, I hope. Now wine and music go together.'

As wine was poured out the man of Kamrup clapped his hands and a curtain at the far end of the hall was drawn apart revealing a neat little stage; and a number of pretty singing girls appeared there carrying various musical instruments.

'Pray go on with your wine,' the host exhorted as he refilled the bowls of his guests. 'The night is still young. Later on, there will be some dancing. If you will excuse me for a moment I shall have a word with the ballerinas. They feel somewhat shy because they have not given a public performance for some time. Of course,' he added, 'you are my friends and they ought to have no scruples before you.'

When their host had withdrawn the Inn-keeper moved closer to the Watchman and noticed to his disgust that he was already sleepy and confused. 'But,' he murmured to himself, 'I am sure I have seen these girls somewhere. Where could it be? Their faces seem familiar.' He tried to think hard and closed his eyes.

And when he opened them it was already day and he was lying on the moss covered flagstones of the empty shell of the ruined monastery hall. The Watchman was there, already up: he was rubbing his eyes and peering at the faded frescoes on one of the walls.

'Look,' the Watchman cried. 'Look! Here are the portraits of the girls who sang for us last night.'

True enough there were the vague outlines of the musicians and the dancers and in a corner was the image of the saffron-robed stranger from Kamrup; he stood apart with a trident in his hand. And near him were a number of painted donkeys and sheep: they were twenty in all.

When the Elder heard their story he did not laugh. He listened in silence that bristled with thoughts. Finally he murmured as he stroked his beard, 'Visions have their origin in those who see them. But between ourselves, the end of the world is not yet at hand.'

The Man who read the Scriptures

THERE was once a simple-souled brahmin called Koolookata-Popeye. Of course his real name and surname were very different. Nevertheless, when he was at school some of his fellows called him, 'Koolook,' and others 'Popeye,' and still others 'Koolookata-Popeye.'

'And,' explained the brahmin to his wife shortly after their wedding, 'now that I am a man I cannot very well shake off the nicknames given me by my school-mates. Anyhow, what's in a name? I don't mind being called Koolookata-Popeye.'

'But I do,' said the wife. 'I don't want to be called Mrs Koolookata-Popeye all my life. And tell me, who will ask a man with such a name for his blessing at births and deaths and marriages?'

'There may be some truth in what you say,' the brahmin admitted; 'but we shall see. For the time being we may live on the dowry you have brought. Mind you, I know the scriptures by heart and can repeat by rote all the aphorisms of our Seven Sages. So,' he assured her, 'there is no cause for alarm. When people are in need they will naturally ask for me. Surely I shall get regular offers and worthwhile invitations. There are not many like me.'

Unfortunately, the wife's fears proved to be true. Our Reverend Koolookata-Popeye was rarely asked to conduct any ceremony. The dowry was soon used up and the wife's patience gave way.

'Now,' she said to her husband one day, 'You go out and seek some work somewhere. I have had enough of your hanging round and mooning and doing nothing but standing in my way. For God's sake, go somewhere, no matter where, but find some way, any way, to get some money.'

The brahmin murmured, 'One mustn't take the name of the Lord in vain.'

And this made his wife more angry. She declared that she was sick of the slick sayings of the Seven Sages and unless her husband went out immediately to find some work she would leave the house and return to her mother. So the poor man was forced to go out as he was, without taking with him anything —not even his scriptures.

'But where am I to go?' he asked himself as he walked north-wards. 'To the Himalayas? To the slope called Manu's Descent? There the ground is said to be strewn with gems because the Seven Sages walked there. So,' he mused, 'there I shall pick up a few precious stones and return home to spend the rest of my days in reading the scriptures.'

He went on and on, not noticing where he was going; for his thoughts were concentrated on the Seven Sages: he walked like one blindfolded, when all of a sudden he stumbled and saw to his consternation that he was on the very brink of a deep shaft, an almost bottomless pit. It was a narrow escape. The mouth of the shaft was overgrown with tall grass and weeds, concealing the danger it presented to all unwary travellers; one step more would have brought him disaster. He thanked his stars, and to appreciate his good fortune and the doom he had averted, he leaned forward and peered into the pit. He was sur-prised to notice a tiger, a monkey, a snake, and a man clinging to its sides.

They too saw him and begged him to help them to get out.

'Sir,' prayed the tiger, being the nearest to the brink and the first to catch his eye: 'Sir, there is great virtue in saving the afflicted. Kindly think of that, and pull me out. Please help me to join my family, and I shall be always grateful to you. You will have no difficulty in coiling a rope with the lianas round the banyan trees here.'

Coiling a piece of rope, the brahmin reasoned, presented no great difficulty; but what he dreaded was the behaviour of the tiger after he had been drawn out of the pit. Was not man the tiger's natural food? 'Moreover,' he told his supplicant, 'you have been without any meal for some time. What would prevent your eating my flesh and drinking my blood as soon as you are drawn out? One of our Seven Sages has said:

Wasted is every gift that goes where it does not fit;
Wasted is service lavished on sluggish mind and wit;
Wasted upon ingratitude is the kindest plan;
Wasted is courtesy on one not a gentleman.

Now think of that. Moreover, I have a long way to go to collect some gems. I cannot really waste time in pulling out a heavy animal like you.'

At this the tiger bound himself with a triple oath promising the brahmin his gratitude. 'Sir,' he then pleaded, 'I am an ignorant animal and cannot argue things out with a learned brahmin like you. But have pity on me and pull me out. I will do my best to recompense you for your trouble. And have no fear about my behaviour. For though uneducated I know:

Of all sins, for ingratitude alone
There is no expiation that will atone.'

This made the brahmin think and finally he reached the conclusion, like the Seven Sages,

If disaster befalls in saving a soul
It spells salvation and a saint's aureole.

'That being the case,' he said to himself, 'I ought to help the poor creature.' And so he pulled the tiger out.

Now the monkey said, 'Holy Father, you ought to help me as well. Surely you have no reason to fear me. And I do promise you recompense when I am freed from this living death in a dungeon.' And the brahmin pulled out the monkey.

The snake then begged to be taken out. She was a female of her species. So, she argued, both chivalry and charity claimed that she too should be saved from her sad plight. At this the brahmin said, 'One shudders at your very name. Your nature is too well known, I am afraid. There's no knowing what you will do to me once you have me at your mercy. You had better stay where you are.' The snake then took the triple oath like

60

the tiger, and said, 'Sir, do you think we bite our victims for mere fun? We are the instruments of Fate. We do what Fate ordains us to do much against our will. However, my triple oath binds me, and you need not have any fear of me.' These words made the brahmin change his mind, and this reptile too was taken out.

All these creatures thanked the brahmin and said to him, 'Sir, the man down there in the pit is a veritable shrine of every evil. Beware of him. Please don't bother about him, but leave him to his fate. The wicked ought to suffer.'

'What makes you think he is wicked?' asked Koolookata-Popyeye.

At this they quoted a saying of the Seven Sages:

> *A man his real self truly reveals*
> *When under calamity he reels.*

Then they added, 'While we three were trying to devise means for getting out of the pit by helping each other, he spent his time inventing stories to put us at loggerheads. Such a man is thoroughly untrustworthy. For

> *We all know well when misfortunes impend*
> *The enmity of rivals must reach an end.*

But not with him! However, Sir, you are better qualified to judge a human being than any of us. So please do what you think best when we are gone.'

The tiger then said, pointing to some nearby hills, 'Sir, do you see the ridge with three crests? It is called Siva's Trident. My home is in a cave in its southern slope. Please do me the honour of visiting my home one day so that I may make some return for your kindness. Surely you would not like me to drag my debt into the next life. So do come soon. My name, by the way, is Broad-Stripes. Just call out for me when you pass by Siva's Trident and I will come out to meet you.' With these words he left the company for his home.

Now the monkey said, 'I live quite near the tiger's cave, by the side of a waterfall known as Monkey's Leap. You can't miss it. So do call for Long-Tail whenever you pass by the site. I am not wealthy and I hate the idea of leaving a debt unrequited. Please pay Long-Tail, that's me, a visit soon.' He then went away.

'My name is Spread-Hood,' said the snake now. 'I have no fixed home like the others. So I can't really ask you to call on me. But in any emergency if you tap the ground three times and call out my name, I shall be by your side.' With this she crawled away.

The man in the pit now shouted impatiently, 'Brahmin! Why don't you pull me out? Have you no sense of duty, no idea of your obligation to a fellow man?'

The gruff tone of this man's voice was enough to put any one off, and had not our brahmin been simple-souled he would not have bothered to listen to all that this fellow ranted on the virtue of practising brotherly love and winning friends. Koolookata-Popeye, however, said to himself, 'Poor man, he is in a difficult plight. So he has lost his temper. He cannot help his voice any more than I can help mine. He should be helped. Perhaps he has a wife who has sent him out to get some money. In that case we might travel together to Manu's Descent. He may have his faults, and who has none?—Not I. The Seven Sages say:

He who seeks friends faultless
Shall for ever remain friendless.

I ought to pull him out without any further delay.'

As soon as Koolookata-Popeye had hauled the man out of the shaft he began shouting and abusing. 'What a fine brahmin you are!' he cried. 'Lending a helping hand to the animals before bothering about me! I have half a mind to throw you in the pit to teach you a lesson. However, let bygones be bygones. I am a goldsmith at Baroch and my shop sign is a Golden Crown. If you have any gold to be worked into shape you must bring it to me and to none else. Now I am off.' So without a word more, without the least gesture of thanks, the goldsmith started for Baroch.

As for the brahmin, he continued his wanderings for some time. But the Himalayas were far off, and he felt tired. So he decided that he was not meant to be a mountain-climber but a stay-at-home, one born to read and enjoy old books. 'By now,' he said to himself, 'I am sure my wife has calmed down, and she would not mind my returning home without any money.'

On his way back home Koolookata-Popeye passed by the waterfall known as Monkey's Leap, where Long-Tail lived. And just to see if he was still remembered by the monkey, he called out, 'Friend Long-Tail! Where are you?' Immediately he found the monkey leaping down from the tree tops to greet him with an offering of luscious fruits. 'These are as sweet as nectar,' Long-Tail said; 'and if ever you need any such fruits please call on me.' 'You have done,' said the brahmin, 'a friend's full duty. Now can you show me the way to the tiger's cave? As I am here I might as well call on Broad-Stripes.' 'I will gladly take you to his home,' the monkey said.

The tiger came running to meet the brahmin and presented him with an exquisite gold necklace and various other ornaments wrought in pure gold. 'Sir!' Broad-Stripes explained, 'A certain prince once came here to hunt, but his horse bolted the moment I roared. The poor rider was thrown off his saddle and killed outright. All that I am offering you was on his person. Please accept my gifts and then go wherever you will.'

So the brahmin took the gold ornaments and thought of the rough-voiced goldsmith of Baroch. 'Surely,' he said to himself, 'the owner of the Golden Crown will help me to get these things sold. After all, my wife needs money. She did not ask me to bring her such heavy ornaments as are worn by men of the princely rank.'

When Koolookata-Popeye came to Baroch he readily found the shop carrying the sign of the Golden Crown. The goldsmith, however, pretended not to recognise him. He behaved rather coldly and asked bluntly, 'What do you want of me?' 'I have brought,' the brahmin replied, 'some gold ornaments, and should like you to sell them for me.' 'Please show me your things,' the goldsmith said, 'so that I may get them evaluated.' When these were produced the goldsmith examined them carefully and said, 'Would you mind waiting here for a few minutes? I must consult my colleagues to find out the exact price of gold just now.' The brahmin readily agreed.

Then, instead of consulting his colleagues, the goldsmith went straight to the police station to denounce our poor brahmin as a thief. 'Look here,' he told the police as he exhibited the gold ornaments to them, 'I have a brahmin in my shop. He is, I am sure, a receiver of stolen goods. Perhaps he is a thief himself. For he has brought with him this set of massive ornaments wrought in pure gold and asked me to get rid of the things at any price. Now,' he went on, 'you arrest him, and give me half of what I am showing you here: the usual reward for helping you to recover stolen goods.' 'Is he a man of Baroch?' they asked him. 'No,' replied the goldsmith, 'not at all. But some of the things he has brought with him were actually made in my workshop for a prince from Somnath.' 'And what has happened to this prince? Have you any idea?' 'The brahmin says he came a cropper one day while out riding. "Thanks to some holes," the fellow brags, "I dug in the fields to make him fall." The prince was killed outright and the brahmin threw his body in a stream after collecting his victim's ornaments.' 'The matter is most serious,' the police said gravely. 'It must be brought to the notice of the King. This brahmin is not a common thief or an ordinary receiver of stolen goods but a regular murderer. The King should be informed immediately.'

When the King of Baroch heard the goldsmith's lying story he issued orders to have Koolookata-Popeye fettered and put into prison. 'This callous murderer,' he told the police, 'deserves the gallows. However, as he is a brahmin, instead of hanging him you should throw him down the precipice known as the Dead Man's Jump. See that he is executed the day after tomorrow, for tomorrow is a holy day.'

So Koolookata-Popeye was taken to prison straight from the goldsmith's shop. No one bothered to explain the charges against him. They called him scum, dog's dirt, and various other uncomplimentary things of this sort. Finally he was asked to name his accomplices.

'A man,' said the chief of the police, 'a man cannot, all by himself, lay traps for killing riders. Who are your friends, do they live in Baroch?'

The bewildered brahmin shook his head: he knew no one in the kingdom of Baroch except the goldsmith. 'And even him,' he added, 'I have met but once. However, he does not recognise me now. And I can't really blame him for forgetting me.'

'Then who are your friends? Have you any friends at all?'

'Of course, I have a few friends. They are very dear to me.'

'Good,' exclaimed the police chief rubbing his hands. 'Very good indeed. Now let us have their names. Do we know them?'

'Most likely you do,' said the brahmin. 'Every school boy knows about them. They are famed all over the world.' He then gave the names of the Seven Sages and declared that they were his most cherished friends, for he derived much benefit from their writings and sayings.

At this the police chief lost his patience and, turning towards his assistants, said, 'Here we have an instance of the tough type of criminals. You may put him on the rack and yet you will get nothing out of him. Even the expression of his face will not change. Look at him! He is as cool as a cucumber though he is going to be executed soon. Fancy mentioning the Seven Sages who died centuries ago as his personal friends. Very soon he may start talking about the sun and the moon and the stars being his brothers and sisters.'

'They really are,' murmured Koolookata-Popeye as though talking to himself. 'Everyone knows the daybreak salutation:

The Moon on my left and the Dawn on my right:
My brother, good morning; my sister, good night.'

He then recited a short stanza by the sage Bhartrihari:

The wise man counts the world as his own:
Neighbours and strangers are bone of his bone.
The sun, the moon, and every star
His brothers and his sisters are.

'There you have it!' remarked the chief of the police to his men. 'The tough type: throw him down a cliff and he will not bat an eyelid. And mind you, he is capable of loving a tiger or a monkey or even a snake more than any man alive.'

They then left him in his cell advising him, as they went out, to meditate on the enormity of the crime, which he had not committed, the crime of setting traps to kill men and horses. The police chief's parting remark was, 'This brahmin is viler than a snake.'

This made Koolookata-Popeye think of the snake Spread-Hood, and he tapped the ground three times calling her by her name; and Spread-Hood appeared at once.

'I am glad,' the snake said, 'you have remembered me in this emergency. It gives me the chance of requiting an old debt. I shall set you free.'

'How will you remove these heavy fetters?' asked the brahmin.

'Very simply,' replied Spread-Hood as she smiled. 'My plan is ready. I am going to bite the Queen. The King dotes on her and will do anything for her sake.'

'For Heaven's sake,' the brahmin cried, 'don't do that! The Queen has done me no harm. Why should you bite her? No, Daughter Spread-Hood, I will not hear of such a wicked proposal. Leave me to my fate, I beg you, and remember the saying:

Do naught to others which if done to thee
Would cause thee pain: this is the sum of duty.'

At this the snake laughed and said that she had no intention of killing or even harming the Queen. 'Only,' she explained, 'the Queen's body will become completely blue with my poison. And then in spite of the charms of all the magicians,

66

conjurors, medicine-men, witch-doctors, and physicians, it will remain blue till you touch her. With your touch my poison will be neutralised. Then you will go free, loaded with rewards from the King.'

Spread-Hood did as she had promised. The moment the Queen was bitten her body changed into deep blue and she dropped into a deathlike swoon out of sheer fright. And a wail of despair rose from the palace. Soon the entire city of Baroch was filled with dismay. The court physicians failed to cure the Queen, and a proclamation was made with the roll of drums inviting all and sundry to hasten to the palace with antidotes against snake bite.

As foreseen, druggists and cheats, doctors and mountebanks, spell-casters and faith-healers, exorcists and seers, and many others rushed to the royal residence, each with his own nostrum. Their charms and ministrations, however, proved ineffective.

The grief-stricken King now promised a handsome reward and immediate release even to condemned prisoners, confirmed poisoners, and convicted murderers if they could cure the Queen. The brahmin now said to his gaoler, 'I think I can heal the Queen.' At this he was immediately released from his fetters and driven to the palace in a magnificent coach, from which he was helped out by no other than the King himself. 'Please cure her, Sir,' the King supplicated, 'and ask your reward.'

The mere touch of the brahmin's hand restored the Queen. At this they all marvelled. He was conducted to a seat of honour and there the King paid him reverence and asked respectfully, 'Sir, you are no ordinary brahmin. Now reveal to me the mystery of the gold ornaments. How did you come by them? And what led you to come to Baroch to sell them?'

'For,' began the brahmin, 'it was written in the book of fate.' He then related the whole story of his leaving home to find gems, stumbling near a dry well, and all his other adventures from the very beginning right to what he called the sordid end.

'Why sordid?'

'Because,' he answered, 'I am a reader of scriptures, and now

67

I have been hailed as a healer, though I know nothing of the art of healing.'

The King now understood everything. The goldsmith was summoned and sentenced for making false allegations, while the brahmin was sent back home with an escort. As Koolookata-Popeye did not care for gold, the King saw to it that his wife should receive regularly a grant from the royal treasury.

'Well,' the brahmin's wife sighed when her husband had finished telling her his adventures. 'Well, perhaps it was written in my book of fate that I should have a husband like you—one who will do nothing but read the scriptures. Do what you like,' she added with a shrug of her shoulders, 'but please don't stand in my way when I am doing the rooms. And for Heaven's sake, don't tell me anything about your Seven Sages.'

The Wonderful Horse

'MY GOOD man!' said the Prime Minister of Anga to a famous horse-coper of Gandhara: 'My good man, what are you doing here at Mathura? Do you never visit the Anga country?'

The horse-dealer replied that he was at the Mathura horse-mart because it was one of the largest in the world and also he wanted to see how his brethren were faring. 'Next year,' he promised, 'I shall certainly come to Anga bringing with me a fine string of horses. Now I am on my way back home. I have sold all my animals.'

'Ask for me at Champa,' the Prime Minister said. 'Champa, you know, is the royal city of Anga. You will have no difficulty in finding me. We need badly a hallowed horse for our future king, the present Crown Prince. You will get your price.' He then added, 'The fair here is big, but it has nothing much to offer to a real horse-lover. I have come to this annual affair for more years than I can remember, yet I have not come across a single hallowed horse. Mind you, a filly or a mare won't do for me.'

The somewhat puzzled horse-dealer then asked, 'Tell me, Sir, what exactly is a hallowed horse? I have been in the trade ever since I was a boy, but have never heard of such a thing. In Anga you must have strange names for our familiar animals.'

At this the Prime Minister of Anga took him aside and whispered, 'A hallowed horse treads the earth lightly. Its hooves raise no dust. Happiness reposes on its forehead, bounty on its back, and joy in its possession. It has thirty-two characteristics.' This list of the thirty-two peculiarities began with the simple term 'all bay,' and ended with such complicated phrases as 'the smoothness of its coat is like that of the moonstone; the tossing of its mane recalls the surging of the ocean breakers; its neighing is like the trumpet's call; its neck is clothed with thunder; and its feet are shod with plumes of fire.'

'Stop, stop!' cried the horse-dealer. 'Sir, I am a plain man of the hills. I find it hard to follow the big words of the learned people of the valleys. But, depend upon it, I shall bring next year five hundred fine blood-horses to Champa and you will choose the ones that please you most.'

When the horse-dealer of Gandhara had gone, the Prime Minister confessed to his suite that he himself had never seen a hallowed horse. All that he knew about it was from hearsay. 'However,' he ended, 'I believe it understands human speech and talks like you and me when it wants to. Moreover, it gives its rider discernment and perspicacity, if not clairvoyance.'

His listeners nodded, but they too thought, like the horse-coper of Gandhara, that it was not always easy to follow the Prime Minister. They felt completely baffled when he declared, 'Such a wonderful horse, you know, might be right in our midst. Only we have not been fortunate enough to identify it.'

However, they all went back to Champa without buying any horse at Mathura and told the King, 'Sire, we should do well to wait for the man of Gandhara. He has promised to bring here next year a string of five hundred blood-horses. Perhaps there will be one suitable for our Crown Prince.'

The next year it was rather late in the season when the man of Gandhara arrived at Champa with his horses.

'I have been exceptionally unlucky on the way,' he complained. 'I was held up for three whole months at Pujita because of the monsoon.'

The delay, however, was mainly due to a mare, which had foaled long before the horse-dealer's caravan reached Pujita. And on the way all the horses slowed their pace because of her little one, so much so that one day our horse-dealer called together his stable-boys and asked them anxiously, 'Have all the animals been lamed? What has happened? We have not yet covered half the distance we usually do every year.'

'We can't make it out,' they said. 'The horses have stopped neighing and won't get into the water till the mare and her foal get in first. Neither will they touch their fodder till these two have had their fill.'

'The fault,' their master said, 'the fault is, I think, with the foal.' And when he heard that it was exceptionally frisky, he added, 'Sometimes a nasty animal is born and its nastiness infects the whole herd. We must get rid of the foal at Pujita.'

At Pujita, however, no one wanted to buy the little foal. And there the poor horse-dealer spent, as has been said before, three idle months fretting and grumbling. For during the monsoon there was no question of pushing ahead with his herd of several hundred unbroken horses. The roads were impassable and the rivers unfordable. So he stopped in a large caravanserai till the season of showers ended.

He roundly cursed the foal at the time of his departure from Pujita as he settled his bills with the serai people and others. To every one of his creditors he said, 'Wouldn't you care to have a lively foal in part payment of your dues? It is a charming little animal with a smooth coat. Well, take it then for nothing, just as a present.'

'No!' was the usual answer. 'No, thank you,' some said, while others scowled: 'Your wonderful little horse is a fine kicker for its age. It is a good biter too. We don't want a calamity in our household. To be plain: all Pujita knows only too well your wonderful foal. Try your luck elsewhere. It is a real Terror.'

However, there was in the city of Pujita one man who had not heard anything about this little horse. He was a potter: an excellent man, but with no knowledge of book-keeping. He liked making attractive pots and jars, and hated the idea of leaving his wheel to collect his dues. Now this man turned up with his bills when the caravan was already on the move.

'My dear man,' the horse-dealer told him, 'I am very sorry. My cashier left Pujita an hour ago. Why didn't you come earlier, like others? What would you like me to do now? Would you care to wait for a few months? I will settle your bills on my way back. What do you say to this?'

'To tell you the truth,' the potter stammered, 'I would not have troubled you at all. But, you see, I have a wife, and it was she who forced me to come out of my workshop with these bits of paper.'

Just at that moment the lively little foal—the cause of the Gandhara man's perpetual headache since its birth—nuzzled up to the potter; it was followed by a trembling stable-boy, pale and fearful lest the young animal should bite off an ear of the innocent creditor or knock him down senseless on the ground. The sight of the foal gave the horse-dealer the idea that he could perhaps fool the potter and foist the animal on him. So he said, 'Look here, friend Potter! Instead of waiting for six months for your dues, why not take this charming little horse, Terror, as payment.'

The potter said that he should like to consult his wife before he could decide. 'However,' he murmured, 'a frisky foal in a potter's home is as bad as a mad bull in a china shop. What shall I do with this animal?'

Meanwhile the foal had started licking the potter's feet like a pet dog, and he felt instinctively an attachment for it. So the bargain was struck. The potter departed with the animal and the horse-dealer sighed, 'Good riddance.'

The potter's wife nearly fainted when she saw the foal. 'My poor man!' she cried. 'My poor man! Is that all you have brought back from the horse merchant? Send this vicious animal to the tanner straight away. Let it be skinned! Don't you know it is called Terror?'

'The poor thing,' the potter murmured. And the foal as docile as ever trotted up to his wife and began licking her hands. 'The poor thing,' the potter repeated. 'Let us keep it as a pet. It has been separated from its mother.'

'In that case,' said the wife, softening, 'let it stay But see that it does not get in among your pots and jars.'

Now the foal showed exceptional intelligence while moving

72

about the potter's cottage. It stepped about his things without breaking anything. Soon it took to the habit of watching its master at work, and one day when he went out to get some clay, it trotted after him. As soon as it saw his sack full it offered its back to carry the load home.

'My dear,' the potter said to his wife that evening, 'I have not, after all, made a bad bargain. Our little Terror is an intelligent creature. In future it will carry my things for me.'

'In that case,' she said, 'we ought to build a little stable for it. It should be fed decently, and we must see that it does not go out on its own and spread terror among our neighbours. You know, no doubt, it is a biter and a kicker as well.'

So there in Pujita the foal remained and gradually grew into a fine horse.

Meanwhile, the Gandhara man's stay in Champa came to an end. Though he sold his entire stock of blood-horses and was satisfied with his profit, the Prime Minister was anything but happy. 'I have spoken,' the horse-coper was told by the venerable premier, 'to each and every one of your pure-bloods and other horses, but not one of them has answered me. These five hundred are, no doubt, good mounts. But I want one which is hallowed.'

'Next year,' the man said evasively, 'I shall see what can be done.'

And when the next year came the Gandhara horse-dealer's stock still failed to produce what the Prime Minister wanted. The following year yielded no better result. Meanwhile, what the wise premier dreaded happened: the aged King of Anga passed away and his young grandson—the erstwhile Crown Prince— ascended the throne, and then the troubles started. 'We won't pay the youngster our dues,' declared the Chieftains with Rajah Ganesha at their head. 'He is young and inexperienced. We shall take him captive when he goes out hunting all by himself. Then we shall decide which one among us should be elected king.'

73

These seditious mutterings and rumours of revolt reached the Prime Minister's ears, and he told the young ruler, 'Sire, you will have to stay indoors till we get a hallowed horse for you.'

'And what will the wonderful hallowed horse do for me?' asked the new King.

'Such a horse gives its rider discernment and perspicacity, if not clairvoyance. It will save you from being surprised by your enemies.'

The young King sighed: he understood nothing of such big words as 'discernment,' 'perspicacity,' and 'clairvoyance.' He murmured, 'In other words, you don't want me to go out all alone. I am to lead a prisoner's life! For it is perfectly clear that such a horse does not exist except in your fancy. How long,' he asked, 'am I to wait till you find one? Can't you get an expert to go through the hundreds of horses in our stables and see what he says?'

'I shall do my best,' replied the Prime Minister.

And not one but a dozen experts were invited to the royal stables; and they being better qualified than the Prime Minister in judging horses soon discovered that one of the mares must have foaled not too long ago a blood-horse bearing all the thirty-two good characteristics of a hallowed mount. 'But where's the foal?' they asked. They then went through the registers and records with scrupulous care. Yet they found no entry for a colt or for a filly of the hallowed kind. So the horse-coper of Gandhara was sent for and questioned, 'Have you by any chance sold any of your foals during the last few years?'

'Not that I know of,' replied the man after consulting his own books. 'No. I am sure I haven't sold any.'

'Have you then given away any?'

'Ah!' he exclaimed, striking his forehead with the open palm of his hand. 'That reminds me of my stay in Pujita. There I gave away a vicious foal to a half-wit. It was the most wicked animal I ever knew. It terrorised the whole caravan. Though a tiny thing it became the herd-leader of five hundred spirited horses.

Not one animal would drink before this Terror had its fill. Neither would they touch their fodder without its permission. No man wanted to have it. But,' he ended with a smile, 'I succeeded, all the same, in foisting it upon a fool of a potter.'

'Have you any idea of the star under which this foal was born? Or precisely where it was born? The exact date? And the hour and the minute?'

'That I could not tell you. All that I know is that it was born somewhere between Gandhara and Pujita. I had nothing but bother till I got rid of it. It brought me ill luck.'

'So,' the experts whispered among themselves, 'that's the horse! It behaved in that way because conch shells were not sounded at its birth. Naturally, no one thought of putting a garland of hibiscus flowers round its neck and marking its forehead with vermilion. What can one expect in such circumstances? A hallowed horse treated like a hack! Anyway, the herd recognised it. We must leave for Pujita immediately and and take silver horse-shoes for Terror.'

The experts from Champa had no difficulty in tracing the owner of Terror in Pujita. 'What have you done with your foal?' they asked the potter. 'The foal you got from the Gandhara horse-coper?'

'Why, it is with me. It carries my sacks of clay and other things as well.'

'Well,' they said, 'we will give you the best ass in the world and a bag of gold. Sell the foal to us.'

'No,' said the potter shaking his head. 'I like my horse, Terror. Why should I give it up?'

'Now, think over our offer. Talk the matter over with your wife. We shall call again tomorrow morning. Perhaps you will change your mind. We shall gladly buy you a pair of asses instead of one.'

The experts did not want to arouse any suspicion about the true value of the horse, and thought they would get it in the long run at a cheap price, especially as the animal was thought to be a real curse by the potter's neighbours and in fact by most people of Pujita.

As soon as the experts had left the horse asked the potter, 'Why don't you press for a stiff price? Here is your chance.'

'Don't talk such rubbish,' said the potter without even looking up: he thought it was his wife who was talking to him and not the horse, Terror. Of course the horse had never spoken to him before, and he had never even dreamt of a talking horse. As he busied himself with his wheel he repeated, 'I don't want to hear rubbish.'

'Where does rubbish come in?' Terror demanded. 'They will pay you any sum you want.'

'Can a man sell his pet or his son for money? Go away! Don't make me angry.'

'But,' said Terror, 'you will make me angry if you don't listen to me. If you had a son destined to be the Prime Minister then would you force him to stick to the potter's wheel simply because you love to see him hanging round here? Would that be fair to your son?'

'Now,' replied the potter, not yet aware of the fact that he was talking to his horse, 'I know I am no good at arguing. Let me get along with my work. I shall do what pleases you.'

The horse now said that a consent forced out of a person was no consent at all: it was an assent dragged out with a sword thrust. An all-bay pure-blood born under a lucky star deserved to serve kings only; its merits made it worthy of the best fodder served in a golden manger. 'Just as a journeyman is worthy of his hire,' Terror went on, 'such a mount is worthy of its keep. Where will you find money enough to buy a gold manger? You should do well to strike a bargain. Say to the men of Champa, "Give me the price of a hallowed horse for my Terror," and you will get a hundred thousand rupees.'

Meanwhile the potter's wife had walked in unnoticed and she interjected, 'In that case it would be foolish to delay the deal.'

The potter now looked up and was bewildered. Whenever

his wife changed her mind she used the formula, 'in that case.' Did she or did she not want him to sell the horse?

'Sell it,' she said as she put her arms round Terror's neck. 'My poor little thing!' she addressed the horse, 'We shall miss you. But where shall we find a gold manger to put your fodder in?'

'All right,' mumbled the potter. 'Two of you are against me. I shall do what pleases you.' (Neither he nor his wife now found it strange that a horse should talk like a man. They were simple and they took everything for granted.)

'It won't please me,' Terror then declared firmly, 'if you ask for less than a lakh of rupees or for as much gold as I can push away with a single kick.'

The next morning the experts from Champa called again on the potter and asked, 'Have you thought over what we told you yesterday? You have. That's good. How much would you like to have for your horse?'

'My Terror is a hallowed mount,' the potter began. 'You must pay me either a lakh of rupees or as much gold as Terror can push away with a single kick.'

This nearly staggered them. They then had a confabulation among themselves. 'The wicked man of Gandhara,' one of them whispered, 'must have warned him.' Another murmured, 'But we must get Terror at any price. That's what the Prime Minister told us. If the rebel Chiefs hear about the horse they will surely offer a fabulous sum.' 'So,' they concluded, 'let us pay a lakh and get the animal straightaway.'

The deal was made. Terror was handed over to the experts, and they immediately had the horse shod with silver horse-shoes.

The stable-boys accompanying the experts then took charge of Terror and brought it to Champa.

The Prime Minister of Anga was delighted, and so was the young ruler. But soon their joy turned into consternation, for they heard that Terror had gone on hunger strike.

Why did Terror refuse food and drink?—None of the stable-boys knew the reason why, though the horse did. 'Would they have dared treat a great pandit with negligence?' Terror mused. 'Would they have received a learned man without due honours? Do they not know that I am a hallowed horse and I have my prerogatives?'

As the horse refused to speak the stable-boys could not read its thoughts. They reported that the much prized mount was fast losing its weight.

'Do something about it,' the young King ordered. 'We must find out what's wrong with our hallowed horse.'

The horse-leeches and farriers attached to the royal stables examined Terror and declared that there was nothing wrong with it. 'Only,' they added, 'it is vicious. Out of sheer viciousness it is refusing food. The coper of Gandhara was right: it is a wicked animal, a born troublemaker. All the horses in the stables have stopped eating on its account.'

Their answer did not please the King, and the Prime Minister hurriedly summoned the experts once again to report on the matter.

And the experts were horrified when they inspected Terror's stall and paddock. They rushed back to the Prime Minister and told him in one voice, 'You have boobies for stable-boys! They have treated Terror as though it were a simple racer or a mere high-priced charger. Goodness gracious! Where is its gold manger? And where were the musicians when it was first brought to the royal stables? And why has not the city been decked with flags in its honour?' They then gave a long list of things which ought to have been done to welcome Terror to Champa.

'The horse seems to be as important as an ambassador,' remarked the young King.

'Indeed it is, Sire,' replied the experts. 'Certainly it should be treated with deference to make it feel at home in its new surroundings.'

'What should we do now?' asked the Prime Minister.

'Do what we have suggested,' the experts replied. 'Also invite the first lady of the land to coax Terror to take its food out of its gold manger.'

They followed the instructions of the experts. Later on the Prime Minister came to the stable and apologised to the horse on behalf of the State for the inadvertent oversight in welcoming it to Champa in a right royal manner. Then the young ruler himself came and expressed his regrets.

All the same, Terror did not unbend, it refused its food! And on account of Terror all the other horses refused their food as well. The experts were consulted again, and they demanded the presence of the first lady of the land. 'Where is she?' they asked. 'She must come out. She must speak to the horse.'

'Ah, where is she?' the Prime Minister sighed. 'Where is our imp?' She had, he gathered, left her classroom to chase some monkeys and had not returned home since then. 'Where could she possibly be?'

A search was made, and she was finally discovered sitting upon a tree munching unripe mangoes and talking to herself: 'I prefer candies.' She was persuaded, much against her will, to be bathed and perfumed and adorned. Finally she was brought before Terror and left there alone with the animal.

'I am the King's cousin,' she said to the horse. 'And that's why they call me the first lady. Isn't that a nuisance? Anyway, the bother won't last long. They say my cousin will get married one day, and I shall cease to be the first lady.'

Terror looked at her and then turned its head away. 'Where are her manners?' the horse wondered. 'She is munching something while speaking.'

'Do you care for mangoes?' the first lady of the land asked. 'I don't really care for them. But I thought you might. So I brought a few hidden in my wimple. Here they are. Take them, if you will. I like candies, and that's why they call me Candy-Cheek. But I have other names as well. They are a bit long and I can't spell them. Can you spell? What's your name?'

The horse pricked up its ears, but did not say anything.

79

'Oh, I am sorry,' Candy-Cheek continued. 'I forgot you are young, so you can't talk. But I am sure when you are as old as Candy-Cheek you will be speaking like everyone else. I am now six and the next year I shall become seven. And then Candy-Cheek will become as old as the Prime Minister.' She then complained that although she was denied sweets Terror had had the privilege of eating as much sugar as it wanted. Not only that: the horse had had its hooves washed with milk and honey! All this she felt was somehow topsyturvy. The world she declared, was upside down: Rajah Ganesha, the leader of the rebels, wanted to marry her and then send her cousin, the young ruler of Anga, to a desert island to die without food and drink, whereas the hallowed horse had plenty of food and drink, yet it wanted to die of starvation.

Now the horse came closer to Candy-Cheek and licked her face.

'Oh,' she cried clapping her hands, 'I am not your manger! But I don't mind being kissed by you. Anyway, lick your manger just once and eat something. Then I shall get some candy. That's what the Prime Minister told me.'

'Well,' said the horse now, 'I shall eat for your sake.'

'So you can talk!' Candy-Cheek danced with joy. 'That's good. Now eat a lot and become strong so that you can bite off an ear of Rajah Ganesha, the naughty man who wants to cut off the head of the Prime Minister. Do you know him? I don't: I have only heard of him.'

'Tomorrow,' the horse said, 'I shall make you a present of Rajah Ganesha's ears.'

'Thank you. But one ear will do. If he loses both his ears he will become deaf. And that would be too bad.'

'Not at all,' Terror assured her. 'He deserves to have his head chewed off. He is the leader of the rebels. I know all about him. He wants to kill the Prime Minister and the King as well.'

'So you know everything. Then why wait for tomorrow? Why not go now to bite off his left ear? And please take me with you.'

'All right,' said the horse. 'But you must go to the Prime Minister first and tell him to get ready to lodge five thousand horses in the stables and five thousand prisoners in the fort. Tell him also that Terror is no longer piqued.'

Candy-Cheek did not have the courage to speak to the Prime Minister. So she wrote out—with great difficulty—a message informing him that she was going out for a ride on Terror's back and that he must enlarge the stables for five thousand new horses and prepare food at the fort for five thousand captives. She then changed into her jodhpurs and put on her riding boots, and finally slank unperceived to Terror's side.

And as soon as she got on the horse's back it shot out like an arrow and galloped straight into the heart of the rebel camp. There it stood still before Rajah Ganesha's tent and uttered a low neigh. Immediately all the five thousand horses of the encampment whinnied back acknowledging Terror as their leader.

Rajah Ganesha and other Chieftains rushed out of their tents to see what was happening. They were overjoyed to see Candy-Cheek in their midst: she was the prize they were anxious to capture. Rajah Ganesha rubbed his hands in glee, crying, 'So Providence is aiding me! Now my friends is the time to strike at that nincompoop youngster who sits on the throne of Anga. I shall marry Candy-Cheek and rule the land in her name. Lift Candy-Cheek down from her horse! Come, Candy-Cheek!' he roared, 'Come inside my tent! Rejoice, my friends, rejoice!'

Now, Terror snorted, and Rajah Ganesha's glee turned into sorrow. For the five thousand horses of the rebels immediately reared on their hind legs neighing fiercely and then fell on their unsaddled riders, seizing them by their belts with their teeth. A minute later an earless Ganesha, held in the jaws of his own mount, saw a whole cavalcade of five thousand proceeding towards Champa with Terror at their head.

And that was how the revolt was crushed thanks to the hallowed horse, called Terror.

'You are a most wonderful horse,' the young King said to Terror as he garlanded it with wreaths of hibiscus while conch shells were blown in its honour. 'You deserve much more than the experts have proposed.'

That evening the city of Champa was illuminated to celebrate the victory wrought by Terror, the hallowed horse. There were fireworks and bonfires as well as music in the principal parks. The Prime Minister gave a long speech in the central square. His address ended with the remarks: 'The First Lady of the Land, Maharaj-Kumari Shrimati Narayana-Datta Raj-Rajendra-Nandini Jayashri Suvarna-Varna Deva-Priya, etc. etc., fondly called Candy-Cheek, will confirm my statement that a hallowed horse gives its rider discernment, perspicacity, *and* clairvoyance. . . . Long live Terror, the most wonderful horse!'

Gokul the Labourer

THOUGH Gokul the Labourer lived in a village not far from Benares it had never occurred to him to visit the Holy City on the Ganges. Indeed he had never thought of venturing outside his village and the field where he toiled.

'It is not normal,' murmured his fellow labourers and blamed the overseer for not paying Gokul enough for an occasional spree in the town.

'It isn't my fault,' said the overseer. 'Gokul prefers to have his wages in kind and not in cash.' And that was true: Gokul insisted on being paid in grain and cloth, sufficient for the food and clothing for his family and himself; and when he needed anything special, he got it by bartering. 'In town,' the overseer explained, 'they want cash. But our Gokul knows it only by name. He has not handled a single coin in his life. You know his refrain: riches and ruin both begin in an "r". I can't force him to change his ways.'

'Well,' they persisted, 'you will have to do something about it. He is strong and healthy, but will soon run to seed if he does not get a holiday.'

So the overseer took Gokul aside and gave him ten shining silver rupees and advised him to take a day off.

'What's the idea?' Gokul cried in indignation. 'I am hale and hearty. Why should I be robbed of a day's work?'

'Look here, Gokul,' the overseer said, 'I don't want to rob you of anything. Only you have been working hard, and that's why you are being given ten rupees as a present and a day's leave with full pay. Now don't come to work tomorrow, otherwise both you and I will get into trouble with your fellow workers.'

'How shall I spend the day then? And what am I to do with these rupees?'

'For Heaven's sake, go to Benares and buy there something for your wife, Ganga; and the ten rupees will be soon spent.'

Gokul thanked the overseer and at the end of the day hurried back home to his wife. 'There, Ganga,' he said as he spread out the money before her. 'There are riches for you!' The good woman's delight knew no bounds, and the children were called in to share her joy. 'Well,' Gokul continued as he contemplated the newly minted coins, 'the next thing to consider is what should be done with this sum. Tomorrow is a holiday for me. And if you do not mind I shall go to Benares to buy something for you and for the children. Now what would you like to have?'

Ganga made a rapid calculation: a fourth of what her husband had received ought to be offered to the High Priest of the Shrine of the Lord of the Universe, and the remainder spent in presents.

'But what presents?' asked Gokul. 'Exactly what? In Benares one can buy anything: an elephant, if you like, or a Wishing Tree, if you prefer.'

'Good gracious!' exclaimed Ganga. 'I thought you knew my taste. I should like to wear a brocaded sari for a change. Benares is famous for its silk. Why not get me ten yards of the very best.'

'And I,' cried the young son, Sishu, 'I should like to have a horse and a sword.'

'Please,' said the little daughter, Bina, 'a red handkerchief and a pair of golden sandals for me.'

'All right,' said Gokul as he bade them goodnight. 'These things will be here by tomorrow evening.'

Though Benares was only a couple of hours' run from his village, Gokul got up at early dawn, said his morning prayers, and taking a stout staff in his hand started on his journey.

When he approached the Holy City his attention was first attracted to its glittering domes and towers. Then he gazed in wonder at the immense flights of stone stairways on the shelved

84

left bank of the Ganges, which flanked the city. Its palaces and pavilions seemed to have been raised not by men but by cyclops. As he passed through its winding streets lined with interminable arrays of balconied buildings he felt himself utterly lost. Finally, when he reached the gate of the sacred shrine—the Temple of the Lord of the Universe—he stood for a while in silent awe, and then gathered enough courage to ask a venerable reciter of the scriptures if he could proceed to the inner sanctuary to offer his prayers and thanksgivings. 'Enter, Son,' said the old man, 'and bestow your alms. For it is written in the scriptures, "Prayer puts a man on the way to paradise; sacrifice leads him to its portals; but these are thrown open only to him who is charitable." Walk in, Son, and say your prayers and make your offerings.'

After worshipping and depositing his offerings, Gokul went to the great bazaar of Benares to make his purchases. And here the thick-pressed crowd of buyers and sellers, touts and loafers, beggars and brokers and hangers-on hopelessly bewildered him. He was no less amazed with the endless arrays of inviting shops displaying ware from every part of the world. He gaped with open mouth at everything he saw, and felt for the first time what an ignorant being he had hitherto been. He thanked his comrades in his thoughts: 'But for them,' he said to himself, 'I should not have come here to spend a whole day watching such marvellous things.'

Jostled by the crowd it took him some time to realise that his sense of wonder was exposing him to unforeseen dangers: more than once he was nearly knocked down by careless porters carrying heavy loads and what was still worse he felt strange hands trying to thrust into his pockets to finger their contents. By and by, the bustle which he had at first admired so much put him out of humour, and he determined to finish his business as quickly as possible and return to the peace and quiet of his village.

So without more-ado he entered a shop which exhibited a rich collection of satins and silks, and demanded, 'I want to have a look at your finest pieces. Mind you, the very best and be quick about it.'

The shop assistant looked at him with puzzled surprise: Gokul's accent and appearance revealed unmistakably that he was a country labourer. 'It would be sheer waste of time,' the assistant said to himself, 'to try to sell such a man anything.' So he hesitated. The manager, however, read his thoughts and took him aside to whisper, 'He comes from the country, my boy. You may judge that from his ear-studs and staff. He must be one of those rich farmers stinking of brass: they stick to the plain ways of the peasants and make a parade of their boorishness. And take it from me, he will go to the King's court dressed as he is without feeling the least bit put off. Why, he will talk to the Emperor of China in the same way as he talks to his overseer. These fellows,' the manager kept on, 'they have guts and they have money. We'll show him some of our finest things.'

Gokul tossed and tumbled every piece of silk in the shop. The things looked extraordinarily seductive. It was difficult for him to make up his mind. Finally he decided upon an orange sari with a gold embroidered hem and edges. 'This will do,' he said, wrapping it up and putting it under his arm. 'Now what's the price?'

'As you are a new customer, Sir,' the manager began in an ingratiating way, 'you will be offered a special price. For we would like you to come to us whenever you honour Benares with your visit. Maybe, you will kindly recommend our shop to your friends and relations. Therefore,' he continued, 'we shall ask only the cost price of the sari—five thousand rupees. For any one else our normal price would be six thousand. Look at the material and examine the exquisite embroidery with gold thread. It is cheap at six thousand, and at five thousand a real bargain.'

Gokul stared open-mouthed and as he replaced the sari on the counter repeated in utter amazement, 'At five thousand rupees a real bargain! Surely, you must be mistaken. Do you mean rupees like these?' he asked as he held out the few coins he had with him.

Gokul's bewildered look astonished the manager. As a rule, he knew from his personal experience, the farmers were great hagglers over the prices asked of them. But rarely had he come across one like Gokul, trying to beat down the demand for five thousands to merely five.

'Certainly,' Gokul repeated as he displayed his coins, 'you do not mean rupees like these.'

'Of course, I do. And I tell you it is cheap at five thousand.'

'Poor Ganga,' Gokul sighed, thinking of the disappointment in store for her. 'Poor Ganga.'

'Poor who?'

'My wife.'

'What have I to do with your wife?' asked the manager, whose tone altered as his chance of sale receded.

'Why,' said Gokul, 'I will tell you everything. I have worked hard in the fields ever since I was a boy and have never handled any money till yesterday, when I was forced to accept ten newly minted rupees. Of these ten, three have been left in the Temple of the Lord of the Universe, and with the remaining seven I intend to buy a sari for my wife, a horse and a sword for my son, and a red handkerchief and a pair of golden sandals for my little daughter. And here you are demanding five thousand rupees for a piece of silk. Tell me,' Gokul ended in a reproach-ful tone, 'how am I to pay you? With what money am I to buy the other things?'

'Clear out of my shop!' cried the infuriated silk-dealer. 'I have been wasting my time and rumpling my silks for a mad-man! Go back to your Ganga and your booby babies. Buy them a packet of candies. And don't trouble me any more.' He then thrust Gokul out without ceremony.

'You can't teach manners to mercers,' Gokul murmured after experiencing similar treatment in several other silk shops. 'They are just rogues and rascals. But there ought to be some decent people among the horse-copers. They at least know the ways of country folks, of men like me.'

He had no difficulty in finding the horse market. And there

the moment he made his wishes known he was surrounded by at least a dozen dealers; and one, stronger and stockier than the rest, forcibly dragged him aside to inspect his equine exhibits: there were several scores of horses. 'Sir,' the man said, 'what sort of an animal would you like to have?'

'A good one,' Gokul replied. 'I want a good horse for my son, Sishu.'

'I understand,' the dealer said. 'But there are horses and horses.' He then gave an astonishing catalogue of names as he pointed to different animals: blood-horse, arab, charger, courser, racer, hunter, roadster, goer, pack-horse, draught-horse, cart-horse, post-horse, shelty, bayard, bidet, mare, filly, colt, stallion, gelding, stud, foal, pony.... 'And then,' he continued, 'certainly you have your own preference for colour. I know of a young farmer who would rather die than ride a roan, and his neighbour is just the opposite: nothing but a roan pleases him even if it happens to be a jade.'

'Please stop,' cried Gokul. 'How can I make up my mind if you confuse me with so many names at the same time. Let me judge your horses on my own, and give me some time to think.'

The horse-dealer now whispered to one of his stable-boys, 'The up-country farmers are tough customers. But they have money. Bring out the black prancer, and let us hear what he says.'

Gokul greatly admired the splendid black horse as it pranced along delightfully before him and was on the point of declaring that his choice was made when a rival dealer sidled up to him and murmured, 'Forgive my butting in. I know this black prancer. He goes well when heated, but is dead lame when cool.' The same man helped Gokul to change his mind when he had nearly decided for a white pony with a long tail. This time he gave his warning to Gokul in signs: from a distance he pointed to the hand of a stable-boy, which was lacking a finger, and then took his own hand to his mouth making champing movement, while looking at the pony which fascinated Gokul. Our Labourer understood the message: such a purchase incurred the hazard of Sishu's losing a finger, for the white pony was a biter.

The mere thought of such a mishap upset Gokul and he ran away from the stocky horse-coper to embrace the rival and thanked him for his timely warning. 'I don't care for biters,' Gokul said. 'As you seem to know a lot about the horses here, can't you suggest a suitable animal for my young son, Sishu?'

'In fact,' the man declared in a solemn tone, 'I do know a lot about horses. But I must be frank with you and tell you straight-away that not one of my own ponies will do for your little son. However, my cousin has a real jewel, the very thing for a pros-perous farmer's son. The trouble is that he doesn't want to part with it. Let me think,' he went on, after a pause, 'let me think. I believe as his boy has been sent to school in Delhi, he may be induced to sell it after all. Can you wait here for a shortwhile? I shall see what can be done to help you.'

Gokul was all gratitude. He blessed his stars for coming across such an understanding man.

In less than a minute a smart little grey pony cantered up, holding its head and tail in the air, and Gokul lost his heart to it the moment he saw it and wanted to settle the deal at once. 'Friend,' he said, 'it is no use wasting any further time. I should like to do a bit of sight-seeing and shopping before I return home. Now what's the price?'

'For any other person,' the man began, 'my cousin would not have parted with this lovely pony for less than two hundred rupees. But as you are my friend, I have persuaded him to reduce the price to a mere one hundred and ninety.'

Gokul stepped back open-mouthed. 'What a surprise,' he babbled. 'Must the horse-copers be as disgusting as silk-mercers? Why, I thought you at least understood the country folks.' He then repeated his story, the same he had recounted to the silk-merchants in the great bazaar.

The man had hardly patience to hear the whole of Gokul's account. 'And fancy,' he cried, 'my throwing away friendship on a fool like you! I have risked a quarrel with one of my breth-ren on account of a bumpkin who does not know the difference between a pony and a donkey! Go back to your Ganga, and buy for your brat a hundredth share of an ass.' He then walked away in a rage, cursing and swearing, and calling Gokul all sorts of names.

Our poor Labourer did not know where to turn to hide his disappointment. He stopped a passer-by to seek his advice, but the man pushed him aside, crying, 'Go away! There are beggars enough in Benares to make one's life hell. But you are the limit. Wanting golden sandals!' Another man advised him to seek shelter in the Charity Hospital for the Mentally Diseased. Finally, some one did direct him to a shop where gold-plated sandals were sold, but the prices were prohibitive.

So, disgusted with his day of adventures, Gokul instinctively turned his steps homewards at sunset. While passing through the suburbs of Benares he heard a stoutish mendicant crying, 'Charity! Charity! He who gives to the poor lends to the Lord! And the Lord repays him a thousandfold!'

'Friend!' Gokul addressed this mendicant, 'Friend, you are the only person in the whole city of Benares with whom I am ready to make a deal. Here are seven rupees. Take them and use them in the name of the Lord, and see that I am repaid a thousandfold. For I do need a big sum to buy a few presents.' He then recounted to the surprised mendicant his story, how he had never touched any money in his life and how his fellow labourers had insisted that he should be accorded a gratuity. 'And that's how,' he ended, 'the idea of buying presents was put into my head.'

The mendicant readily accepted the money and promised to pray for Gokul, assuring him: 'The Lord returns a thousandfold whatever is given in his name.'

When Gokul returned home he found every one waiting for him though it was rather late. 'Where is my horse?' asked Sishu; 'and the sword you promised me?' 'And my red hand-kerchief and the golden sandals?' demanded Bina. Poor Gokul shook his head and said nothing.

Ganga understood there was something wrong and so she

said to the children, 'Look here, it is time to go to bed. Shops in Benares are not the same as our grocers. In Benares people do not carry about their shoppings with them. Shop-keepers have porters, and these porters bring home what you buy. They will bring the horse and the other things here later on. Now you run to bed.'

'What happened in Benares?' Ganga asked when the children had withdrawn. She listened patiently as Gokul recounted his journey step by step, and nodded her approval to everything he had done till he came to his meeting with the portly mendicant. She then sat up and interrupted his story. 'You did not,' she said, 'I hope, lend him anything.'

'In the name of the Lord,' Gokul replied, 'I did. Benares seems to be full of cut-throats and rogues. He was the only honest man I came across. He promised me before many witnesses a thousandfold return. What more do you want?'

'You will drive me mad,' Ganga wailed. Her lot, she lamented, was harder than that of any other woman in the world because of Gokul's absurdities. It was sheer lunacy on his part to refuse wages and insist on payments in kind only. Half of her time was wasted each day in jogging about from one place to another, exchanging corn and cloth for the hundred and one things needed for their home. Did he think that housekeeping in the circumstances was easy? If so, he was welcome to look after the house while she replaced him in the field. 'In God's name,' she finally burst out, 'what have I done to merit a husband like you? Can't you understand a joke?'

Gokul shook his head. He failed to understand what she was driving at.

'Can a man buy a brocaded sari for ten rupees?' she rated. 'And a horse and what not? I thought you would buy a wooden horse and a toy sword for Sishu and for Bina a pair of slippers, and maybe, a few knick-knacks for the house. Have you no common sense?'

'Then,' asked aggrieved Gokul, 'why did you advise me to buy ten yards of brocaded silk to begin with?'

At this Ganga flared up: her patience was exhausted. And in spite of the lateness of the hour she ran to the overseer's house to complain about her domestic troubles.

And the next morning the overseer gave Gokul a new task, that of digging a well, all by himself, near a disused gravel pit. 'This will,' the overseer told him, 'bring you to your senses. A man must show some common sense in life. I am more sorry for Ganga than for you.'

Gokul, however, did not complain. He worked harder than ever, and the well was finished earlier than the overseer had expected. This resulted in his getting a new bonus and a day's leave.

'Go and spend the day in Benares,' the overseer counselled.

'And,' said Gokul, 'what am I to do with the bean-shaped pebbles I found in a big jar when digging the well?'

'Eat them!' replied the exasperated overseer. 'And if you can't eat them, sell them. Use some common sense, my man.'

Gokul felt hurt at the curt reply of the overseer. He tried his teeth on the bean-shaped things and found them inedible. What was he to do with them? It then occurred to him that he had seen similar stones in a shop window in Benares.

So on the next occasion of his visit to the Holy City he went straight to this shop and asked its owner, 'Would you care to buy some of the bean-shaped stones you have in your window?'

'Certainly,' said the man. 'I shall pay you a decent price for each. How many have you got?'

'I have a cartload,' Gokul replied. 'But, mind you, I want in exchange a wooden horse and a pair of girl's slippers.'

'A cartload!' The man laughed. 'You are joking. Just show me one of your pebbles.'

At this Gokul produced a handful, which so surprised the jeweller—the shop in question was a gem-seller's store—that it was some time before he could speak. He became pale, for he thought Gokul was perhaps a robber or a bandit who had rifled a treasure chest. 'Will you stay here, sir,' he finally stammered, 'for a few minutes till I return.' So saying he left the shop with trembling feet, but reappeared soon afterwards with a number of armed constables and their officer, while a large crowd, avid for sensational happenings, gathered outside the shop.

'He is perhaps,' said the jeweller, pointing at Gokul, 'the escaped convict the Governor is looking for.'

The turn of events made Gokul speechless. His surprise became greater when he saw the stout mendicant, who begged in the name of the Lord, step forward and declare, 'I am sure he is the man. He throws away rupees by the handful.'

'Hang him! Hang him!' the crowd now shouted. 'He must be the bandit who has killed many an innocent pilgrim. His pockets are bulging with gold and silver.'

Gokul got no chance of explaining anything. The constables wrenched his staff off his hand and then fettered him. He was shoved in a closed wagon and brought before the Governor of the nearby prison. There he was introduced as an escaped convict who was under death sentence.

'Welcome, Sir Bandit,' the Governor said to Gokul in a sarcastic tone. 'Welcome back to your prison! It was charmingly gracious of you to bestow a handful of rupees on a beggar. Your generosity aroused his suspicion. And he has helped us to trace you. This time you are not going to escape.'

'What have I done?' asked bewildered Gokul.

'What have you not done, Sir Bandit? You have robbed and murdered, and have been justly sentenced to death. Had you not escaped you would have been hanged long ago. Now,' the Governor continued, 'there is only one thing I should like to know from you, if you would be so kind as to explain it to me: why on earth did you want to exchange a cartload of precious stones for a toy horse and a pair of slippers?'

'For Sishu and Bina,' replied Gokul and related his story about the gratuity of ten rupees, his first visit to Benares, and all the rest.

The Governor became uneasy. Evidently Gokul was telling

the truth, and at the same time a score of people affirmed that he was no other than a condemned convict who had escaped from his cell. What should be done? Finally, the Governor decided that the King should re-examine Gokul's case.

The King was sitting with the High Priest when Gokul was brought in. To every one's surprise both the ruler and the prelate immediately stood up and murmured, 'There he is! There he is! The man we have been looking for.'

The High Priest put his arms round Gokul's neck and said, 'Son! Where have you been hiding yourself all these days?' The King too embraced him and ordered that a most splendid shawl should be put on his shoulders. Refreshments were served to him.

'Both the King and I,' the High Priest continued, 'we two have had the same dream for a number of nights. A voice told us that the Lord wants us to help his devoted servitor, Gokul the Labourer. Then in our dreams we saw you toiling in the fields, digging in a gravel pit, going about your village, saying your prayers. But our dreams gave no information about your address.'

Dumbfounded Gokul did not know what to say.

'And then,' the King began, 'I saw clearly in my dream that you wanted to buy a piece of brocade for your wife, a horse and a sword for your son, and a red handkerchief and a pair of golden sandals for your daughter. These things have already been procured for you as well as other gifts. Now tell me where you come from, and our presents will be immediately sent to your home.'

Gokul gave his address and added that a wooden horse and a toy sword as well as a pair of simple slippers would perhaps be more suitable for a man of his condition.

'No, no,' the King protested. 'We cannot disobey the command we have received in our dreams.' And the High Priest said, 'There will be a real horse as well as a wooden horse for your son, and for your daughter a pair of golden sandals as well

as a pair of ordinary slippers. Otherwise I shall fail in my duty.'
'I am extremely sorry,' the King added, 'for all the troubles you
have had to go through. And please don't object to the things
that have been chosen for your wife.'

'Please tell me,' Gokul now said, having recovered his self-
composure, 'please tell me only one thing: why did the jeweller
make such a fuss over my bean-shaped stones?' He then produced some of the pebbles he still had in his pockets. 'These are
nice and smooth. What's wrong with them?'

'These are priceless gems.'

This information upset Gokul. 'What shall I do with gems?'
he asked himself, and then proposed to the King, 'Sire, let me
make a deal with you. In exchange for your gifts you will have
to take the cartload of my gems. A fourth part of the gems
should go to the Shrine of the Lord of the Universe. Gems,'
he added, 'may bring blessing to those who know how to use
them. I don't. You see, my mother told me, "Blessed is the
man who has found his work; let him seek no other blessing."
I have found my work and I love my work. What need have I
of gems?'

When Gokul returned home he found the King's gifts already
there.

'Thank God,' Ganga said to him as she embraced him, 'thank
God, you told the King right things, and did not make a fool
of yourself before the High Priest. I have already heard all that
took place in Benares.'

'Ganga, stretch your legs according to your coverlet. That's
plain common sense.'

The Jackal that fell into a Dyer's Vat

A jackal fell in a dyer's vat
  And changed his coat to blue;
The beasts all said: 'A marvel, that:
  And what a noble hue!
Give him the crown, the royal mat!'
  So there, his form all blue,
His sire disowned, the jackal sat.

'ACCORDING as Your Highness commands!' the animals of the forest said as they prostrated themselves before him, not knowing that All-Blue was just a plain jackal that had fallen into a dyer's vat while prowling about the out-skirts of the neighbouring town. 'What noble complexion,' they said to each other in admiration of their newly elected king. 'We have never seen his like before.'

Our jackal, now known by the name of All-Blue, did not want the animals to have anything to do with his brethren lest they should find out that he was not of any ancient lineage. So he decreed that all jackals should be debarred from his court. Not only that, from the forest as well.

A certain old jackal, seeing that the rest of his tribe were very much cast down, said: 'Don't be downhearted! Should it continue in this way, All-Blue will force us to be revenged.'

'Easier said than done,' muttered the others. 'Where are we now going to live? In the town, which is full of dogs? And be torn into shreds? Let alone the question of revenge! All-Blue has all the animals on his side.'

'Then let me alone contrive his downfall,' replied the old jackal. 'Can't you see that the lion, the tiger and the rest who pay him court are taken in by his outward appearance? They obey him as their king simply because they are not aware that he is nothing but a common jackal. We must do something then by which he may be found out. Now this is my plan: we should get together in a body at the close of the evening and set up one general howl in his hearing. And I warrant you, the natural disposition of our race will force him to join us in the cry. For, it is said:

Hard it is to conquer nature: if a dog were made a king
'Mid the coronation trumpets he would gnaw his sandal string.

And the animals, discovering that he is nothing but one of us, will feel thoroughly ashamed of themselves, and execute him on the spot.'

The plan was carried out, and everything happened as the old jackal had foretold:

Your nature is a thing you cannot beat;
It serves as guide in everything you do;
Give doggy all the meat he needs to eat
He cannot still help gnawing at a shoe.

The Crane and the Gander

A GANDER that came from the land of cockaigne
    Was hailed by the leader—a Magadhi crane—
    Of birds breasting Hooghly's renowned muddy drain:
'From where have you come, friend, what sort of domain?'
'My stream is delightful: it is in the south.'
'What pleasures refined does it give to the mouth
Of such birds as we?' 'Oh, it never knows drouth:
It's crystal clear, nectar sweet, wine to the mouth.
All golden the lotuses: riverain banks
Are covered with blooms, and no plebeian planks
But glittering stones ornament its wide flanks,
Adorned with gilt images all placed in ranks.'
'But tell us how fine are the snails over there?'
'Snails! Sorry, there are none. For such I don't care.'
At this the crane's laughter rang loud through the air.

Tell me who was wiser:
The crane or the gander?

An Outing with King Vikram

'LET US go out this evening,' said King Vikram of Ujjain to his aide-de-camp,' and see for ourselves how things are.'

'Very well, sire,' replied the aide-de-camp. 'I shall be at your disposal as usual at midnight.' King Vikram had the habit of making, after dark, a circuit of his capital, attended by only a single guard, in order to inform himself of the temper of his subjects and also to become better acquainted with the details of their lives. This habit, however, was not much encouraged by the Prime Minister, for on more than one occasion the King had got into scrapes. 'And,' according to the Prime Minister, 'the poor P.M., that's me, had to pay the piper. See,' he advised the aide-de-camp, 'see that the King does not take undue risks. After all, each citizen lives according to his status and means. Remember, young man, I shall hold you responsible if anything happens to the King. Make no mistake about that.' The aide-de-camp thought about the Prime Minister's warning and asked King Vikram, 'Sire, what disguise do you propose for this evening?'

'I leave that to you,' replied the King. 'Anyway, I intend to visit the area outside the city walls. Therefore, we must go out of Ujjain before the city gates close on the stroke of twelve, and stay out till dawn. What do you say to that?'

'That should be all right. But, sire, if you do not mind, you will have to be disguised as my servant.'

'Why?'

'Because you have the habit of telling the truth and nothing but the truth everywhere. And this nearly led to your murder when we got into the thieves' den the other night.' At this the King laughed. But the aide-de-camp declared solemnly that it was a narrow escape. 'For,' he explained, 'fortunately the chief of the thieves thought you were joking when you said, "I am the Chief of Ujjain, King Vikram in person." I should not like such a thing to happen tonight. If you are asked any questions I shall answer them on your behalf. I have no scruples about white lies and cock-and-bull stories.'

'All right,' said the King. 'Have it your own way. You will be my master and I shall be your man from midnight till dawn.'

They went out through the West Gate disguised as travellers from Java and struck the road leading to the great port of Barigaza. As they roamed about they found nothing unusual. The calm of the moonless night reigned everywhere, broken only by the chimes of the hours and half-hours of the citadel of Ujjain and the occasional barking of watch dogs and the hooting of owls.

'Let us go to some inn,' suggested the aide-de-camp. 'This is a dark night. There is nothing much to see. As the city gates won't open before dawn we might as well try to get a few hours' sleep. Tomorrow you have a heavy programme, sire.'

'Listen!' the King interrupted. 'I hear strains of music coming from a cottage over there. Who at this hour can be amusing himself in such a poor quarter? Let us go and see what's happening.'

They found the cottage in question in a sad state. In fact it was no cottage, but an isolated, miserable hut. The fences round it had broken down; the walls were crumbling, and a stream of light issued from one of the fissures.

'When the outside is so sadly dilapidated,' the King murmured, 'the state of affairs inside must be still worse. Yet the inmates are singing gay songs!' He looked in through a chink and saw inside an old man weeping, a young man in mourning engaged in singing, and a shaven-headed nun—or a widow: he could not tell which—busy dancing. 'Have a look,' he said to the aide-de-camp, 'and explain the mystery to me. Or ask the owner of the house to explain it.'

The aide-de-camp demurred. 'They are having fun,' he said, 'in their own way. It would not be fair to disturb them. After all, have we any right to probe into their private affairs?'

The King wanted to have his curiosity satisfied and simply refused to be dissuaded. He called out for the owner. And hearing his voice the young man in mourning immediately came out and asked, 'Who are you? What do you want at this hour of the night?'

'We are travellers from Java,' said the aide-de-camp. 'We are looking for an inn. Could you please guide us to one?'

'This is a poor quarter. There are no inns here. And my home is a house of mourning; so I cannot invite you in.'

'But,' King Vikram interrupted, 'you are singing gay songs, all the same.'

'How does that concern you?' retorted the young man in mourning. 'You should not busy yourself with other people's affairs.'

'When things are as they should be,' the King replied, 'no man has the right to interfere in other people's affairs. But as you are in mourning it is everybody's duty to keep the vigil with you.'

'At least,' the aide-de-camp now broke in, 'this is how we understand things in Java. We leave happy neighbours to themselves: we go to them if they invite us; but we force ourselves on those who are unhappy so that we may share their sorrows and lighten their burden. So,' he continued, 'you will excuse my man for what seems to you unjustified curiosity on his part. In truth, it is not curiosity, but anxiety that has prompted him to put his question.'

'In that case,' began the young man, 'I cannot refuse him his request though, I fear, no one can lighten my burden of sorrow. My story in brief is this. My father used up all his resources in giving me a costly education: he wanted me to be a court scribe. But as no post has fallen vacant for a long time no competitive examination has been held, and naturally I have no job. Today for no reason in particular my father said to my wife, "Go daughter, and get a silver bowl immediately; for I am sure a royal guest will be calling on us soon." And she, having no money, sold her superb tresses to get the bowl. Now, as you see, it is long past midnight and my father's expected guest has not arrived. The old man is weeping. "Because," he says, "on account of a silly dream I have made my daughter-in-law shave her head for nothing." And my wife is dancing simply to distract him, while I am singing for the same purpose. But the old man refuses to be consoled. Now,' he ended, 'you have heard my story. The night is nearly over, and I must ask you to leave me. You will have no difficulty in finding your way to Ujjain. The silhouette of its citadel looms in the horizon.'

'Sir,' King Vikram said, 'I have never heard of such family loyalty and devotion to each other as obtains in your household. You have an able mind and I do believe that you will be among the candidates at the Literary Examination tomorrow.'

'Literary Examination!' the young man exclaimed. 'What examination?'

'Why, sir,' the King replied, 'the competitive examination for a vacant post in the King's court,' 'That's why,' the aide-de-camp added, 'we are hurrying to Ujjain. In fact, that is the object of our long journey from Java to Barigaza and from Barigaza to Ujjain.'

'I have not heard of any examination,' murmured the young man.

'Whether you have heard or not,' they expostulated, 'you should sit for the competition. You owe it as a duty to your father.' With this they left him.

And the next morning, soon after the chimes of the bells of the citadel had announced the beginning of a new day, King Vikram issued orders for holding a competitive examination. The criers spread the news rapidly throughout the city and then beyond the city walls. Surprised scholars said to each other, 'Fancy as late as last night we did not know anything about this examination. But for the official crier we might have missed the news altogether. Well, better late than never.' And they flocked to the Great Hall of the University.

The young man who lived in the tumble-down hut went with other candidates to the Great Hall. 'Imagine,' he said to his wife while preparing to go out, 'imagine, men from distant Java knew about the date of the examination; and we, living a stone's throw from Ujjain, came to hear of it only by accident. I had better hurry. Meanwhile, you may tell father when he wakes up that the visitors of last night were perhaps of princely, if not royal, ranks. And do please keep your head covered so that he may not think of your lost tresses. In our community, as you know, only nuns and widows have shaven crowns.'

When a big gong was sounded in the Great Hall and the candidates were seated, the aide-de-camp announced the subject of the examination essay, proposed as was the custom by none other than the King himself. The theme was an unusual one: Reflections on the songs of a young man in mourning, the hopes of a shaven nun dancing, and the thoughts of an old man weeping.

Of all the candidates none, save one, knew how to present a coherent statement, let alone an essay, on such disparate subjects linked together. And this man knew through his sad experience what to write and he wrote well. The examiners were unanimous in recommending him to the King for the post of the court scribe.

'So,' the young man told his wife, 'King Vikram has accepted me. But how did he come to know that you have a shaven head? For when I was presented to him he congratulated me and said, "Now you can afford to buy back your wife's long tresses." Isn't that strange?'

Garib and the Forty Thieves

SITARA was the prettiest bride of the city of Bijapur. But her beauty brought little joy to the home of her husband, Garib the Sandal-maker. For she was bone-lazy.

Each evening when Garib returned home after his day's work he found her sitting idly, all by herself, gazing vacantly at space with a face as long as a fiddle. And, of course, nothing was ready. This was trying for a poor man who counted much upon his wife's help.

'What's the matter, Sitara?' he asked her once.

'Oh, nothing,' she replied languidly. 'I am day-dreaming, or star-gazing, if you will.'

One day Garib lost his patience and gave her a piece of his mind. 'Enough of it, Sitara,' he stormed at her. 'I don't mind your day-dreaming, or star-gazing, if you will. But why on earth can't you do your dreaming and gazing in my shop instead of mooching in the back-yard? All Bijapur will then flock to the place, and I shall do a roaring trade.'

'That's precisely what I don't want to do,' she replied pettishly. 'I am sick of being a sandal-maker's wife.'

'What would you like me to do, turn cobbler? Or write poetry?'

'No,' she cried. 'For Heaven's sake, no. Do something decent.' She then burst into a flood of tears and ran into the kitchen. Drying her eyes, she placed before him, a few minutes later, some of the richest dishes Garib had ever tasted.

Garib was so taken by surprise that he did not know what to say. He was fond of his young wife, indeed proud of her: she was comelier than the fairest beauty in the King's palace. It broke his heart to see her snivelling and not taking the least morsel from her own plate. What was wrong with her? He finally asked, 'Aren't you taking anything?'

'No,' Sitara replied. 'I wish I were dead. I have no need for food. If you cared for me you would have read my thoughts.'

'Between ourselves,' Garib said, 'I am neither a thought-reader nor an astrologer.'

'That's the trouble with you,' she snapped. 'If you cared for me you would take to astrology. And my days of misery would end.'

That was a new surprise for our sandal-maker.

Sitara knew well that her husband was too fond of her to refuse her anything. So she had bidden her time and got together some of the different articles she thought a regular astrologer needed for his profession: a number of old almanacks, a counterpane printed with the signs of the zodiac, an astrolabe, an abacus, a pair of compasses, a few sea shells, and prayer beads.—This curious assortment, which she believed would be useful to her husband, was now presented to him. Garib was frightened. He complained that he knew no more of astrology than of wizardry. Had he been asked to take to some handicraft he might not have demurred. But astrology! That was beyond him.

However, Sitara was adamant. She wanted him to be an astrologer and nothing else. For she had seen the Court Astrologer's wife in the market place and she was covered with jewels. People stared at her though she was homely, while they hardly noticed Sitara in spite of her beauty. 'If only,' she pleaded with her husband, 'you were less stubborn and did what I am telling you, everything would be all right. I shall look after the sandal shop and you will go tomorrow to the market place with the things I have bought for you. I have even retained a nice booth for you.'

Garib still remonstrated, but in vain. Sitara wept and declared that she would return to her mother unless he did as he was told. This settled the issue.

The next morning Garib's friends were surprised to find him sitting in a booth right in the heart of the market place. He was wrapped in a curious counterpane bearing the signs of the zodiac. Near him was a big board covered with bold letterings:

'Fortunes told! Nativities calculated! Horoscopes interpreted!'
'The poor man,' they said, 'the poor man has gone off his head.
Otherwise he would not have abandoned sandal-making to
make a fool of himself in the market place. No man can become
an astrologer overnight. The science of stars demands a life-
time of hard study.'

Soon a big crowd gathered in front of Garib's booth and
various rumours circulated. 'He had a dream last night,' some
said, 'and in his dream the Goddess of Wisdom bestowed on
him the gift of fore-knowledge.' Others said, 'He is stark mad.
He should be sent to an asylum straightaway. Perhaps it is not
yet too late to cure him.' 'You are mad yourselves,' Garib's
defenders declared, 'and you should stop slandering him. How
do you know he is ignorant of astrology?' 'We know him well.
He is Garib the Sandal-maker,' 'That proves nothing,' retorted
those who believed in the efficacy of dreams: 'You are simply
jealous of him. Krishna was a herdboy who looked after cattle,
but that did not prevent him from destroying demons. You are
mean-minded. Clear out of this place before we drive you out.'

The crowd grew more dense and the excitement increased.
It looked as though they would come to blows on account of
Garib. At this juncture the arrival of an unexpected client of
our amateur astrologer eased the situation. The client happened
to be no other than the august Court Jeweller, Laddu Singh.

Laddu Singh was in great distress. For he had lost the richest
ruby belonging to the King's crown. Every search had been
made to recover this gem of inestimable worth, but all to no
purpose. As the loss could no longer be concealed from the
King, the Court Jeweller knew that his fate was as good as
sealed: the usual punishment for stealing—or losing—a crown
jewel was death.

In this hopeless state—the condition of a condemned convict accorded a brief respite—Laddu Singh was passing by the
market place when he overheard a bystander speaking to his
neighbour: 'Don't you know Garib the Sandal-maker? He has

been inspired in a dream and turned astrologer. He foretells the future.'

A drowning man clutches at a straw, and no sooner did Laddu Singh hear the word 'astrologer' than he was off: he fought his way through the throng surrounding Garib's booth, and introduced himself to our erstwhile sandal-maker. He recounted Garib his tale of woe. 'If,' he finally said, 'you truly understand your art there ought to be no difficulty in your recovering the lost gem. Do your calculations and give me the result. If you succeed in tracing the ruby I shall give you two hundred gold pieces. But if within six hours I don't get the result I shall use my influence at court to have you punished as an impostor.'

Our poor Garib was thunderstruck. Had Laddu Singh deigned to wait for a few minutes to give Garib time to recover his speech he would, no doubt, have heard from Garib's own lips the circumstances that had led him to put on an astrologer's counterpane. But now it was too late: Laddu Singh was gone.

Garib reflected on his misfortunes, the irony of fate that the one for whose love he had garbed himself as an astrologer should be the cause of his impending imprisonment. Gathering up his paraphernalia, he cried aloud, 'Oh, woman! Oh, heartless woman! Have you no pity? Do you wish your husband to drown himself in the Bhima river? Is life worth living when one has lost face?'

'Please,' just then whispered a veiled woman, coming close to Garib and interrupting his monologue, 'Please do not speak so loudly. I will offer you four hundred gold pieces to keep your lips sealed.'

Garib started. In his distraction he had not noticed the coming in of this woman. Who was she? What did she want? Why was she on her knees before him? The mystery was soon solved when she began her confession.

'Have pity on me,' she implored. 'Please do not reveal to my husband that it was I who stole the ruby. It would mean disgrace and divorce. You are a married man and you should know that women love jewellery. That ruby is so lovely that I wanted to have it for myself. I did not know that it belongs to the King.' Anyway, she guessed that it was extremely costly, and that was why she was following her husband about, wearing a thick veil, to find out what he was going to do. The moment he turned his steps towards Garib's booth, she felt she was lost. 'So,' she ended, 'I waited till he was gone to talk to you. It was kind of you not to have revealed the truth to him straightaway.'

Now Garib assumed all the dignity of a true seer, and in a solemn tone declared, 'Woman, I know all that you have done and much more. However, it is lucky of you to come here in time to confess your sin. Now run home and put the ruby under the mattress of the couch on which your husband takes his mid-day siesta. Remain satisfied that your guilt will never be disclosed. And do not forget to bring me the promised four hundred pieces of gold within an hour.'

Needless to add that Garib gave the Court Jeweller the precise location of the missing ruby and got the stipulated fee. Earlier he had received a bag of four hundred gold pieces from the Jeweller's wife. So he ought to have felt happy. But his heart was as heavy as lead when he returned home at sunset: for he considered it was not right for him to dabble in a profession which was not his.

Long before his arrival home the news of his success as an astrologer had been noised about, and Sitara received him with open arms: she was not the Sitara of yore—the languid woman with a long face—but a bright, lively thing, a perfect housewife who had everything ready to welcome home her tired husband.

'There,' said Garib, drawing her aside, 'there are several hundred pieces of gold in this bag: money enough to buy you a jewelled diadem. And, I hope,' he continued, 'for God's sake, you will not ask me to hazard my life again in this unholy business of astrology.'

'Come and have your food first,' she said and fed him with unheard of delicacies, while he recounted his adventure in the market place hoping she would understand his dilemma and never again ask him to pose as an astrologer. 'I know no more about stars,' he ended, 'than you do about the happenings in Cathay. For an ignorant man like me it is dangerous to profess any knowledge of the planets and their influence.'

Garib's account, however, had an altogether different effect from what he had expected. 'My dearest husband!' Sitara exclaimed, 'How can you think of giving up your new profession? You haven't given it a fair trial. Your very first day's earnings have been more than a life-time's profit from sandal-making.'

Garib protested: sandal-making was honest work whereas a pretence to astrology was downright swindling. Did she want him to become a thief in order to make more money?

His remonstrations were, however, useless. Sitara began sobbing and complained that he did not love her. She threatened she would return to her mother that very night. A bag of gold coins was worth less than a single ruby. And she wanted so much to have some decent jewellery. If he cared for her he would not have denied her the satisfaction of owning a treasure-casket. 'You are welcome,' she finally declared, 'to invite any hussy to do your housekeeping. I am now going.'

So in the end Garib gave in.

The next morning a crowd bigger than that of the previous day gathered in front of Garib's booth. But they were not noisy nor quarrelsome. They all bowed in silent awe as Garib took his seat behind his counter. They kept their distance and gazed on him in blind admiration: for the story of the ruby had gone abroad and spread his fame as the ablest astrologer ever seen in Bijapur. Every one in the market place was loud in praising his virtue, though each man had his own version about the discovery of the lost jewel.

'I know it for a fact,' a puppet-seller proclaimed, 'Garib the Seer consulted his almanacks and then his astrolabe to find the position of Saturn. The bearings of this distant planet revealed the precise location of the lost ruby. It was hidden by a magpie under a basil plant in the Court Jeweller's garden.'

A grain merchant was meanwhile telling a different tale to a broker: Garib had no need to consult the almanacks, for he knew the position of the stars by heart; his discovery of the missing gem was due to his power of meditation. 'And,' the merchant added, 'this power Garib has gained through a dream. The ruby, by the way, was accidentally put in a jam pot by the Court Jeweller himself.'

'Garib,' according to a dyer, 'had a look at the nativity clock of Laddu Singh and told him straightaway that the ruby was in a mousehole. He also advised him not to take onions on full-moon nights if he wanted to avoid similar troubles in future.'

They were all talking in this way when the wife of the richest Jain merchant of Bijapur happened to be passing through the market place in her palanquin. 'Who is Garib?' she asked her maid, 'And find out why they are all talking about him.' She was soon informed about the discovery of the lost ruby and about a hundred other miracles which, needless to say, had never been performed by our Garib. At this she immediately alighted from her palanquin and dismissing her maid and bearers, went straight to the Astrologer's booth, elbowing her way through the surrounding throng like one possessed.

There with her face veiled she addressed Garib as 'My reverend father and protector of the unfortunate,' and begged him to help her. 'I have a most jealous husband,' she said, 'and surely he will make my life unbearable when he finds me without the emerald necklace he gave me last evening.'

'Humbug,' Garib muttered without bothering to look at the Jain lady. With downcast eyes he was saying to himself, 'I am no astrologer, but a humbug, a big humbug.'

Hearing the word 'humbug' the Jain lady burst into tears and confessed that she was not always a paragon of virtue and deserved the epithet of humbug. But what was she to do? She had not given away her necklace to any of her poor but deserving admirers. In fact it was round her neck only an hour ago when she left her house for bathing in the Bhima river. But now it was gone. If she returned home without this precious ornament her husband was likely to think that it had been given away to one of her many hangers-on.

Garib was much touched by her candour, and recalled the saying:

The wealthier a Jain grows
The greater he jealousy shows.

But what could he do to help her? He at last turned his gaze on her pityingly and immediately jumped to his feet, crying, 'Good gracious! Look after that rent.' For he now noticed that though the Jain lady's face was veiled, her diaphanous robe was rent from midriff to feet: it was torn while she was pressing through the crowd and exposed her limbs in a most indelicate way. Were her husband here, Garib reasoned, it would have meant murder. 'And Sitara will eat my head off,' he said to himself, 'if she gets an inkling of such a visitor to my booth.' Without more-ado he hastily divested himself of his astrological counterpane and wrapping it round her, whispered, 'For God's sake, look after that rent first. Do hasten.'

These words had a magic effect on the Jain lady, and she rushed off to get hold of the first cab she came across.

Garib was greatly relieved to see her depart. But this feeling of relief did not last long. He was soon seized by a fit of ague. What excuse was he to offer Sitara for the disappearance of his counterpane? 'Will she understand,' he asked himself, 'that I sacrificed it to cover a distressed woman's shame? Most likely not. Sitara's nagging has stopped me from making sandals for feet smaller than hers. She will surely make a scene and will go to the Jain lady's house to make things worse. To be exposed as a humbug is nothing compared with the scandal over an unknown woman who has a jealous husband.' Other thoughts came to his mind and his shiverings increased. 'What would happen,' he mused, 'if the Jain merchant accused him of tearing his wife's garment?' This train of ideas gave him a headache and he closed his eyes.

And when he opened them he saw before him the Jain lady

with her husband. At first he could hardly believe his eyes and bit his fingers to make sure that he was not dreaming a nightmare. He was mystified to notice them bowing deferentially at him. As he stared at them the Jain nudged his wife and she placed a gift bowl filled with pearls on the counter along with the astrological counterpane lent to her an hour ago.

'Reverend father,' the Jain began as he put a bag of coins by the side of his wife's gift bowl, 'I have seen many holy men, but you are holier than them all. Others charge fees before they give any advice, but you advise without asking for any recompense. Here are our humble gifts for you. We are most grateful.'

'What have I done to merit all this?' asked Garib in blank bewilderment.

'Sir,' the Jain lady said, 'do not refuse our gifts. If you do so it would bring us bad luck. You asked me to look after the rent, and I did so. It was in the rent of the tree trunk where I had hidden my necklace before getting into the river. The moment you uttered the word "rent" I recollected exactly where I had put it.'

'You deserve your fee, sir,' the Jain merchant added, 'though you have not asked for it.'

Garib realised in a flash his good luck. His diffidence was gone, and in a bold way, worthy of a high priest, he declared, 'I don't accept any gifts from a man who is unjustly jealous of his wife and whose fate is nearly sealed.'

This came as a thunderbolt to the Jain merchant. Was it written in the book of Destiny that his ruin was imminent? Could nothing be done to avert the calamity? Could not Garib initiate such ceremonies as would propitiate Fate and avert all misfortune? 'Do please,' he begged on his knees, 'accept the price of ten emeralds and save me from disaster.'

Garib raised his price for conducting the rites to avert the evil eye, and his terms were readily accepted. 'All right,' Garib finally said as he wagged an admonishing finger at the Jain merchant. 'All right. I shall do what is necessary provided in future you treat your wife with due consideration. You must never suspect her of any infidelity. Now receive my blessing and return home in peace.'

After their departure he too left the market place, thanking Providence for the bounty he had received and for the boon of saving his face. Though his profit was much higher than that of the first day, he made the resolution not to return to his astrologer's booth any more.

'I have had enough of it,' he said firmly to Sitara as he handed over to her the gifts he had received from the Jain couple.

'Poor dear,' Sitara murmured as though talking to herself. 'Poor dear, you are tired. You have been working hard. I have prepared a perfumed bath for you, and your dinner is nearly ready. It is wicked of me to make you work yourself to death.'

The next morning Sitara, who was so meek the night before, became her usual self. This time, however, she did not cry when her husband refused to return to the market place. She simply said, 'All right, you stay at home or look after the sandal-shop, if you will. I am going to the astrologer's booth to replace you. I shall put on your costume. Now,' she demanded, 'lend me your turban.'

'What!' exclaimed the astonished man. 'You are mad, Sitara!'

'No more mad than you,' she retorted with a toss of her head. 'Do you think a handful of pearls and a few emeralds are adornments enough for a woman like me? You are mistaken, my dear. I may not be a beauty in your eyes, but certainly I am not as ugly as the Court Astrologer's wife.'

'There will be a riot in the market place.' Garib protested, 'if you turn up there dressed as a man. Have you no feelings for me?'

'And where are your feelings for your poor wife? If you loved me you would return to the market place and continue with astrology.' Then she broke down and began to sob hysterically.

And poor Garib returned to his booth to avoid further discussions with her.

He did not know that immediately on his arrival there he was to be invited to the house of the Court Astrologer: this arrangement had been made by Sitara herself.

A chain of events, it should be noted, by chance placed Sitara in a position to negotiate with the Court Astrologer's wife, and she made the most of it. A band of robbers had broken into the royal treasury and removed forty chests of crown jewels and every effort of the police to detect them had failed. The keeper of the treasury, hearing of Garib's recent successes in dealing with lost gems, had appealed to the Court Astrologer for help; and the latter had made his calculations and exhausted his art to no purpose. The news had reached the King's ears, and naturally had evoked his wrath. The Court Astrologer thus found himself in a tight corner. All this was known to Sitara, though not to her simple-souled husband, and she on her own initiative had sent a friendly message to the Court Astrologer's wife, suggesting that Garib might perhaps be of some service at this juncture.

And that was how Garib came to be taken from the market place to the mansion of the Court Astrologer. There he was conducted to a seat of honour and treated with every deference, while a big gathering of high officials watched the proceedings as the Court Astrologer's guests and witnesses.

'Brother Garib,' the Court Astrologer said, 'I am honoured by your presence in my humble home. The ways of heaven are, as you know, at times inscrutable: the high are often cast down and the humble lifted up. The whole universe is under the sway of Fate and Fortune. It is now my turn to sink and yours to rise.' He went on in this way for some time, using flowery language and finally announced to Garib's dismay, 'From now on you are the Chief Astrologer of Bijapur, and I am only your assistant. The King has graciously approved of this arrangement provided you succeed in tracing within forty days the thieves and the treasure chests they removed without leaving the least clue.'

Garib babbled that he knew nothing of astrology; but his protests were in vain.

'It is rumoured,' the Court Astrologer said, 'the thieves consulted you before making their raid. This may or may not be true. But it is your duty to help us all. If you refuse you are likely to be arrested by the Chief Constable for a close interrogation. Mind you,' he added in a low voice, 'our Chief Constable's method of interrogation is as good as butchery. So for your own good, let me tell you that you must find the stolen chests within forty days—the time-limit accorded to you by the King. Now go home and begin your calculations.'

On his return home Garib began packing a few articles for travel in a bag, for he intended to run away from Bijapur to Golconda and open a shop there.

'What has happened?' asked Sitara.

'Believe it or not,' Garib replied, 'I have just managed to avoid the clutches of the Chief Constable. As soon as it gets dark I shall leave Bijapur. Meanwhile you should quietly return to your mother and wait there for my news from Golconda.' He then told her of the task imposed on him. This was, of course, no news to her, and she began giggling. 'Are you stark mad?' cried Garib. 'Is this the time for chuckling? If I stay here I shall be executed after the fortieth day from today. Think of that.'

'My poor husband,' Sitara said, 'Why must you think of running away? Find the thieves and the chests, and then become the permanent Chief Astrologer of Bijapur.'

'Easier said than done. How am I to find the thieves and the chests? Talk sense, my silly girl.'

'Why, by the same means that helped you to find the ruby and the emerald necklace.'

Exasperated Garib was ready to tear his hair off his head. What made Sitara think that it was astrology that helped him to trace the lost things? She smiled incredulously as he repeated that it was mere chance—and not any knowledge of the influence of the stars—that brought about his success with the ruby and the emerald necklace. She started to cry when he elaborated his plan of settling down in Golconda. This time her tears did not tempt Garib to change his mind.

'You are stupid,' Garib rated. 'I must go while the going is good.'

'Listen!' Sitara burst out, 'I have been looking forward to the day when you will be made the Chief Astrologer. Now I don't want to be let down. With a little bit of goodwill and the help of the almanacks, surely you will find the thieves. As for your running away,' she went on, 'I shall see to it that you don't. I am going even now to inform the police about your plan.'

Garib became dumbfounded.

'My good looks,' Sitara kept on, 'mean nothing to you. If I am in rags or lustre, it is all the same to you. If I am dead or alive, it matters little to you. All that you can think of is yourself and nothing but yourself. Now, let me make it clear to you, I am not going to let you stir out of the house for the next forty days.'

To prevent Sitara from rushing off to the Chief Constable, Garib agreed to do as he was told. He resigned himself to his fate. 'Lord,' he prayed in silence, 'let the last remaining forty days of my life be peaceful. Though I am innocent I am going to be charged with the crime of helping thieves to steal crown jewels, and I know I am going to be executed at the end of forty days. Help me to bear my trials with fortitude.' He then asked Sitara if she would do him a favour as he was no good in calculating dates.

'What is it?' she asked.

'Please buy me forty dates. And give me one each day so that I may put the stone in a jar. By counting the stones each evening I shall then know exactly how many of the few days I have to live are gone.'

'I will get the dates straightaway,' she said. 'But let me repeat, if you escape I shall allow myself to be hanged in your stead.'

She then went out, carefully padlocking the house door behind her though she knew there was little likelihood of Garib's trying to run away during her absence.

'Forty,' Sitara said to herself as she stepped out of the house. 'Forty and no more.'

'Sitara!' the neighbour's wife called out. 'Sitara! We have heard the good news. Your husband is now the Chief Astrologer of Bijapur.'

'Forty and no more,' Sitara murmured and, then turning to the neighbour's wife, said, 'Please, sister, remind me when I leave you, "Forty, and not one more, not one fewer." I forget things so easily.'

'Forty thieves! So your husband has already started his calculations! Forty and not one more, not one fewer! How surprising.'

'Now,' Sitara said, 'forty thieves or forty beggars, it is all the same to me so long as I can remember "forty." Sister, are you good at remembering figures? I am absolutely useless.'

The neighbour's wife confessed that she was no better than Sitara in recalling exact figures: it was a man's job. And then turning to a ragged beggar—a street violinist—by the roadside she called out, 'My goodman! You will get a penny if you remind us "Forty" when we have finished our chat. Remember, "Forty and not one more, not one fewer." Is that clear?'

At this the beggar, who was no street violinist, took to his heels as though the magic word 'forty' implied the risk of his arrest and interrogation by the Chief Constable.

'How annoying,' said the ladies as they noticed the beggar running away. They were dying for a nice gossip and at the same time afraid of forgetting the precise number of dates for Garib. So there they stood, in front of Garib's house, talking to each other and repeating loudly, from time to time, 'Forty and no more and no fewer.' One would have thought they were insane.

Meanwhile, the beggar, who was a spy of the gang responsible for the theft of the treasure-chests, came running to his comrades and exclaimed, 'We are lost! Garib has started his calculations and has discovered that we are forty.'

'Nonsense!' said the leader of the gang. 'A frightened man hears what's uppermost in his mind. Let someone else go to Garib's house to do some eavesdropping. Meanwhile, let me tell you that I have raided many an astrologer's home in my time, and not one of them has yet been able to discover my whereabouts or retrieve his stolen property. So don't be nervous. We must, however, lie low for some time. It is prudent to be careful.'

He was talking in this way when the second spy of the band came there and reported, 'We are all found out! Garib's wife has told her neighbours that we are just forty, no more and no fewer. It is God's truth. Garib is a true seer.'

'It needs no astrology,' said the gang-leader, 'to guess that we are forty. Forty chests are missing, one man for each chest. Garib has made an obvious hit. That's all. Anyway, it would be wise to keep an eye on him.'

'What about leaving Bijapur for good?' some of the thieves said.

'That is out of the question,' the second spy announced. 'For Garib's wife has had a talk with the Chief Constable and all the exits of the city are being carefully watched.'

At this the gang-leader ordered one of the men to go to Garib's house as soon as it became dark. 'Try to listen,' he said, 'Hear what he says to his wife, that will give us some clue.'

Now Sitara's zeal to help the police had frightened her poor husband into complete silence. Therefore the scout of the thieves, sent out for eavesdropping after dark, heard nothing at all for a long time; later the half-audible murmurs of Garib's evening prayers reached his ears.

His prayers over, Garib was given the first date by his wife, and he said, 'Ah, Sitara, here's one of the forty. Note well, this is the first, the very first, of the forty.' To this Sitara snapped,

'So what? Do you wish me to shout this precious information from the house-tops? Yes, I know, this is the first one of the forty, and there are thirty-nine others.'

Hearing these words the spy of the thieves raced back to his comrades to announce, 'This Garib is a terrible fellow! The moment he had finished his incantations he discovered my presence and told his wife, "Here's the first one of the forty." We are all lost.' This man's account was, however, discredited by the hardened gang-leader, who declared as before, 'Our fears lead us to hear fantastic things. Anyway,' he added, 'two of you will go there tomorrow evening, and hear what Garib says.'

The next evening Garib said his prayers as was his custom. These, the two spies thought, were magic formulas; then they heard him exclaim, 'Sitara, tonight there are two!' And Sitara, much peeved, retorted, 'Yes, one and one, twice one will naturally make two. You must be a great mathematician to make this tremendous discovery after a whole day's mumblings! There are still thirty-eight.'

At this the astonished thieves fled and told their still incredulous chief what they had heard. So three men were sent on the third evening, four on the fourth. It went on in this way till on the fortieth night the entire gang came to surround Garib's house to hear what he had to say. On that occasion Garib cried, 'The number is now complete! The whole forty are here! The end is now at hand! Tell me, Sitara, did the Chief Constable propose the gibbet or the axe?'

'Isn't that all the same?' Sitara replied in a bored tone. 'What difference is there between hanging and head-chopping?'

At this every member of the gang began to tremble, and they then withdrew silently to their hiding place for a confabulation. There they rated their chief: Garib was not like other astrologers who pocketed their fees before making their predictions; therefore it was no use comparing him with the common run of fortune-tellers and horoscope-casters. 'It was silly,' they cried, 'not to have tried to bribe him earlier. Everyone knows that he has taken to astrology simply because his wife wants some jewellery. Therefore,' they proposed, 'we should try to make a friend of him by sharing with him a part of our accumulated booty.' To this the gang-leader now readily agreed.

They then returned to Garib's house bearing with them a heavy load of jewels and ornaments, and timidly knocked at his door.

The poor sandal-maker thinking that the police had come to lead him to execution cried out, 'Have patience, friends! I know what you have come for. But the deed is unjust and wicked.'

'For Heaven's sake,' Sitara complained, 'don't wake the neighbours with your loud cries. Let me sleep in peace during the night. There is no quiet during the day with your mumblings and prayers. Now go with these men to the place of execution and have done with it.' (Of course she knew well from the Chief Constable that Garib ran no risk of being punished even if he were taken to the place of execution: hence her complete indifference.)

Garib, however, was deeply hurt to hear her talk in this way. But the effect of Sitara's remarks was infinitely greater on the leader of the thieves, and he whispered as soon as the house door was thrown open by Garib: 'Most wonderful man! Most incredible astrologer! We are fully convinced that you know what we have come for.'

'Of course, I do,' said Garib. 'And who can blame you for coming here? You are but instruments of Fate.'

'That being the case,' the gang-leader mumbled, 'I have a proposal for you. Here is a bag containing jewels and ornaments. It will be yours provided you swear to speak nothing more of the matter.'

'No,' exclaimed Garib. 'I won't hear of such a disgraceful proposal. Do you mean to say that a gross injustice should be committed without my complaining about it? Without making it known to the world? I am a patient man, but there is a limit to my patience. I must draw a line somewhere.'

'Have mercy upon us,' pleaded the thieves, falling on their knees.

'A crime is a crime,' Garib kept on. With the bitterness of an innocent man condemned to death, he declared that no crime was made less heinous because it was committed in the dark. 'So,' he said, 'may I know why you have come in the middle of the night? You were expected only at dawn. And why so many when one would suffice?'

'Oh, sir,' the gang-leader said, 'we will restore the royal treasures, but mention us your fee for saving our lives. You are a professional man. Is there any harm in offering you a fee? We won't dream of tempting a man of your standing with a bribe. But surely you have the right to draw your line somewhere on the table of astrological calculations. Why not end your computation with the recovery of the treasure chests?'

Garib started. Only by now he realised that the men before him were thieves and not the agents of the Chief Constable. So he raised his voice and condemned them in a grave tone. 'Guilty men!' he said, 'Wicked thieves! At last you are convinced that you cannot escape the searching vision of one who knows the position of every star in the heavens. However, your timely repentance has saved you. But you must restore immediately all that you have stolen from the King's treasury. And swear from now on you will stop stealing anything of value save gold-plated and jewel-studded sandals of my own making.'

The thieves took the most solemn oath to keep their promise. They were then instructed to place the forty chests in a disused bath house in the royal pleasure gardens by the Bhima river.

'See,' Garib enjoined, 'see that not a single article is missing. You have still a few hours of complete darkness to finish your task. Come back and tell me when everything is done.'

When Garib was brought before the King to give the results of his astrological calculations, he said, 'Sire, through God's grace I have succeeded in getting partial results only. Your majesty will have to choose between the thieves and the treasure-chests: Providence will grant only one or other. We cannot have both. So please make your choice.'

'In the circumstances,' the King said, 'I choose the treasures.'

'And the thieves are granted a full and free pardon?'

'Yes, provided nothing is missing from the treasure chests.'

'In that case, Sire, allow me to conduct you to the royal pleasure gardens by the Bhima river. And the Chief Treasurer should bring with him a complete inventory of the contents of the chest.'

The treasure chests were found precisely where the thieves had left them following Garib's instructions. There was no need to make an inventory of their contents, for the coffers were exactly in the same condition as when stolen, with the Treasurer's seal on them unbroken. Everyone was delighted. They raised shouts of joy in honour of Garib.

'Now,' said the King, 'what reward would you like to have, Friend Garib? Ask and it shall be yours.'

'Sire, issue a rescript,' Garib begged, 'debarring me from practising astrology and let my wife be informed about it immediately. A shoemaker should stick to his last and a sandal-maker to his bench.'

'It is a strange request,' the King said, 'but it will be granted. And from now on you will be the Court Sandal-maker.'

Sitara bowed to the King's decision; but now she had enough jewellery to make any woman envy her, and this in spite of Garib's keeping back the major portion of the contents of the bag he received from the thieves—he needed gold and gems for the exquisite sandals destined for the dainty-footed ladies of the Court.

Sitara, by the way, ceased to be lazy. She became a perfect housewife. 'A good wife,' people used to say when they saw her: 'A good wife makes a good husband.'

Once in Benares

ONCE IN Benares a young student, hailing from Vardaman, had a strange adventure on the very day of his arrival there.

When walking along the river bank towards sunset, he was accosted by a stately matron with a benign smile. Obviously she guessed that he was a stranger: for she asked him straight-away, 'Stranger, are you looking for something?'

Her question upset the young man. For what reason he did not know, the thought then uppermost in his mind was the gold teeth of a bitch mastiff he had come across barely an hour ago in one of the more secluded parks of the Holy City: the mastiff was engaged in fighting with a greyhound; and as there was no one about he had to separate the two; the greyhound ran away yelping while the mastiff stood where she was snarling and baring her teeth. She had four gold teeth. And the smiling matron had the same number of gold-plated canines. This was a curious coincidence. The very thought of it made the student stammer. With considerable difficulty he finally stuttered that he was looking for the greatly renowned Observatory of Benares. For he was a candidate for the Entrance Examination of the Observatory.

His embarrassment made the matron laugh heartily. 'But,' she said at last, 'Young man, you are going the wrong way.'

The student confessed that he was not familiar with the Holy City, having arrived there only recently. 'A couple of hours ago,' he added, 'to be precise.'

'That explains it,' she murmured as though talking to herself. 'Otherwise,' she said as she stared at his feet, 'who would think of walking in his shoes along the sacred Golden Strand of Benares.'

The student mumbled his apologies: he did not know that the entire length of the stone-encased river bank was holy. Of course, he had heard of the Golden Strand—the famous ghats or the flights of steps of massive blocks of gold—leading from the upper reaches to the bed of the river. However, he was unaware of their precise location. As it was the time of sunset everything looked golden, and he had foolishly assumed that the ground under his feet was just orange-coloured stone whereas it was, in reality, solid gold. He felt most awkward.

'Now come with me,' she counselled, 'before they get hold of you and punish you for your indiscretion. Ignorance is no excuse for law-breaking. Here they don't like law-breakers: whether you are a visitor or a resident, it is all the same to them.'

The young man was grateful for her timely warning and thanked her cordially, especially as she offered him hospitality in her home. She must have been, he guessed, fairly well-to-do; for the house she lived in was a substantial stone structure, surrounded by a high wall. The student was accorded a neat, well-furnished room on the ground floor, overlooking a cobbled inner courtyard with a fountain in its middle and a thatched tool-shed in a corner.

'You may stay here, Young man,' she said, 'as long as you like. It won't cost you anything. Only you must not bring in any visitors. I am a recluse, as you can see, living here all by myself. By the way, you may call me by my first name, Matrika.'

It was an ideal room for a student. As the young man of Vardaman knew no one in the Holy City, he gladly accepted her offer and readily assured her that as he was her guest he considered it his bounden duty to respect her wishes.

Though his bed was comfortable the young man had very little sleep that night. Perhaps it was the change of atmosphere, or perhaps the rich dinner his hostess served him, or perhaps the worry over the test examination to which all aspirants to the Observatory were subjected, or perhaps the memory of the four gold teeth of the mastiff—he did not know exactly what—kept him wide awake; he lay tossing in his bed counting the hours.

It was long past midnight when a low whinny of a horse just

outside the main gate of the house made him sit up, and he began debating within himself, 'Should I or should I not get up to drive that animal away?' The horse now neighed, and he heard his hostess call out, 'One minute, Chandrika! Tonight it will be a fight to a finish. I am coming.'

Who was Chandrika? A bell kept ringing in his head: he had heard the name somewhere. Obviously, it was the name of the horse outside the gate; but apart from that, was there someone or something called Chandrika? Then in a flash it occurred to him that Chandrika was somebody whom his hostess detested. For, he recalled, during the evening meal he was asked, 'Tell me, why did you give the glad eye to Chandrika?' 'To whom?' was his surprised response. 'To Chandrika?' 'I don't know her. Who is she?' His puzzled looks must have assured his hostess that he knew no one of that name in Benares or elsewhere, and when he pressed her for further information about Chandrika, she shrugged her shoulders and muttered, 'Don't bother about her. She is a bitch. She is always running after young strangers. Do you recall the greyhound you petted in the park? Well, she is Chandrika. She will get it from me one of these days.' Was Chandrika, he now wondered, a common name for bitches and mares in Benares?

His musings, however, came to an abrupt end when he noticed his hostess walking across the cobbled courtyard and sprinkling herself with the water of the fountain. There was a bright moon, and her every movement could be watched from where he was. He saw her divest herself of her shift and then go the toolshed—or was it a kennel?—to take out a tablet, from which she read out certain strange formulas. She then thrust the tablet back into the thatch of the shed. And afterwards she turned her face to the moon, and then to his horror he found her transformed into a round-bellied black mare. A moment later she trotted out of the house using a side-entrance.

Evidently she was a sorceress. Prudence counselled the young student to leave her house at once. But the sight of a human being changed into an animal was so frightening that it took

him some time to recover the use of his limbs. Finally he totter-
ed out of his bed and without bothering to collect his things
staggered out of the house. Once out in the street he felt better.
But where was he to go? He thought of his examination in the
morning—the examination for admission to the Observatory.
He needed some rest. But where could he find a bed for the
remainder of the night?

It was all quiet in the streets: there was no trace of any watchmen anywhere nor of any stray revellers. Benares, as everyone
knows, is a city of mazes of intersecting streets and lanes and
blind alleys. Our student wandered about for some time in the
hope of coming across a rest house or a caravanserai, but he
found none. . . . Finally, he heard what seemed the sound of a
thunderous applause, and he decided to let the clamour guide
his steps.

But as ill luck would have it, he found himself eventually in
the very park where he had witnessed the dogfight shortly after
his arrival at Benares. And there he discovered that the sound
of the prolonged applause was nothing but the noise raised by
the hoof-beats of two mares engaged in a deadly struggle: one
of them was his hostess disguised as a round-bellied black mare
with four shining gold teeth, and the other, a lean bay, was
most likely Chandrika, the erstwhile greyhound now transformed into a spirited mare. It was a dreadful sight. The mares
shook their manes and bared their teeth; they reared on their
hind legs and then dashed against each other; they galloped
furiously, running in circles, and trying to climb over each
other, and then rolling on the ground to put the opponent off
her guard. They fought mercilessly with their teeth and heels,
with biting and kicking, but without whinnying or neighing.
It seemed as though they did not want to raise too much noise
lest the sleeping city should wake up and stop their struggle.

However, the sound of their hoof-beats soon brought the
night watchmen in their scores to the park, and the young
student slank away, though still trembling in every limb out
of fright.

To end the story, our candidate from Vardaman did not do well at the test examination of the Observatory. His failure, he thought, was due not to his sleepless night but to the gibe of one of the guards, who exclaimed, 'Good heavens!' the moment he heard where the young student had spent his night—his very first night—in Benares. 'Good heavens!' the guard repeated. 'Must every one who comes from Vardaman fall for a sorceress in Benares? One of your Vardamani pandits,' he went on, 'was once changed into an ox by your kind hostess. Fortunately, her rival, Chandrika changed him again into a human being. Otherwise he would still have been chewing cud in a cattle-shed. Young man, you must be pretty blind not to have seen through your hostess at a glance. Astronomy,' he ended, 'is not meant for those who cannot see. Why not try your luck at the Entrance Examination to the School of Philosophy. There are quite a few philosophers who are as good as blind.'

Our young student did not try to get into the School of Philosophy at Benares, but went to Ujjain to study astronomy. On his way he came across a yogi who taught him the art of walking on water and various other extraordinary things. It would, however, take too long to recount them here.

The Woodcock that Refused to be Fooled

'I AM PRETTY,' said Pussy, 'Now don't you agree?'
To the Woodcock, in safety, perched high on a tree.
'True, you are a bird whose bright plumage is fine,
But shy, I should say, and unable to shine.
Just fancy, in fright from me turning away
As though I were really a foul beast of prey!
No reason at all why you should be shy
As no one is near us to watch or spy
How tenderly sweet, pretty Pussy can play
With a beautiful wild bird, if only she may.
Oh, Talk to me! Fly from that very high loft,
Feel my coat: it's pure fur and so silky and soft.
You're afraid still, my poor dear? O, what a shame!
But I swear to be gentle to you, all the same.
Do look for yourself: I have four velvet paws,
While you have got nothing but one pair of claws.
How happy you'd be to take me for a wife
To give you a pleasant and leisurely life,
With children in plenty and a lovely large house.
Now climb down! Don't behave like a cowardly mouse!'
    'Oh, no!' said the wise Woodcock, shaking his head:
'Go and fool some young silly vain crow in my stead.'

When an enemy flatters, it's wisdom to be
As deaf as an adder: now don't you agree?

Lionel's Foster-Mother was a Lioness

A LIONESS was once found walking into the palace of the King of Kanchi bearing a boy on her back. The sentries made way for her: they had been apprised beforehand of her arrival. And she walked straight into the King's private apartment and said, 'Here is your son, Lionel. I am now leaving him in your care.'

'Can he manage without you, his foster-mother?' asked the King.

'Remember the pact we made,' said the lioness, 'when we first met. I was to make the motherless boy as brave as a lion, and then you were to take him in hand. I have done my best. Now,' she ended, 'it is your turn to give him the best possible education suitable for a prince.' She then left the palace to return to the forest where she lived.

And the King of Kanchi, after long reflection, decided to consult his friend, the King of Benares, with whom he had shared rooms as a student in the University of Taxila.

'Send Lionel to Taxila,' wrote the King of Benares in a letter sent posthaste. 'My son, Sura-Sen, is already there. Let the two lads share the rooms which were once ours. I am sure Taxila will make a man of him.'

And that was how Lionel was sent to the oldest university of the world, and there he finished his studies with Sura-Sen of Benares and many other scholars from all parts of the country and even from such distant lands as Korea, Cambodia, China, Siam, Mongolia, Iran, Arabia, and Ethiopia. He returned from Taxila to ascend the throne of Kanchi, his father having died a short time before his final examinations. There was a period of official court mourning, and then came the formal celebrations of Lionel's coronation and afterwards the normal routine as the new King of Kanchi.

'My dear man,' said Lionel one day to the palace chef, 'I am getting a bit tired of your vegetarian dishes. We are no longer in mourning. You should put some variety in our menus.'

'Certainly, sire,' replied the chef and then added rather hesitatingly that it would be of great help if he knew the favourite dishes of Lionel during his university days in Taxila.

'For Heaven's sake,' Lionel burst out, 'don't talk of Taxila to me. Boiled rice and vegetable curry and once in a blue moon a pancake! That was what I got there. Plain living and high thinking may suit the priests and the professors, but I prefer to be highly fed and plainly taught.'

'Very well, sire,' said the chef and withdrew to consult his wife. She advised him to try out a few fish dishes as well as some meat. 'Though,' she added, 'it has been the tradition of the House of Kanchi to be strictly vegetarian, you should not forget, my dear, his foster-mother was a lioness.'

The chef's wife was right. The next day Lionel devoured the meat dishes greedily and increased the chef's salary. Later on, the man was congratulated on the excellence of his cooking and told, 'My dear fellow, I am not a cat. So don't give me any fish. And I have already told you that I don't care for vegetables.'

The chef consulted his wife again, and she said, 'Give him only meat dishes.' And this was what he did to Lionel's great delight. 'Now,' he was told, 'Stick to this menu.'

'But,' the chef asked his wife, 'what am I do when the month of the Autumn Moon comes? You, know, no doubt, no meat is served then in our kingdom.'

'Consult the King,' she advised. 'Try to find out if he cares for venison and pheasants; and lay in a good store in the underground vault where ice is kept. Then there is the possibility of cheating him with mushrooms. And if the worst comes to the worst one can always give him dog's meat.'

It was true, dogs were not debarred from consuming meat during the month of the Autumn Moon, and the tradition of Kanchi allowed butchers to sell offals for dogs to regular customers. A thousand-year-old custom, nevertheless, demanded that the dog owners should present their licences; for even carrion unfit for human consumption was strictly rationed. No one, however powerful, could violate this unwritten law of the four meatless weeks without courting the danger of death or permanent exile.

The poor chef trembled as he explained the state of affairs to his master on the first day of the month of the Autumn Moon. 'Sire,' he added, 'I can, however, prepare mushrooms in such a way as to give you the taste of meat.'

'Mushrooms!' Lionel wrinkled his nose in disgust. 'I don't want to be poisoned with toadstools! Keep them for yourself. But what about my fine pack of hounds? Feed them on rice and curry, and get hold of their meat for me.'

To cheat the king's dogs of their ration proved a far more formidable task than the chef had foreseen. First, they were exceptionally intelligent; one would say they could read the chef's thoughts, and then they were no ordinary dogs but phenomenal hounds as big as asses. Their growl was more terrifying than Lionel's and their voracity for meat no less than their master's. From the first day of the month of the Autumn Moon the whole pack became suspicious and dogged the chef's steps, never giving him the chance of stealing the least morsel from their supplies.

Meanwhile Lionel's appetite steadily increased. His hunger became ravenous, and the huge stock of venison and pheasants laid on the cold storage was consumed even before the end of the first week of the meatless month. The chef was in a terrible predicament.

'If I steal any of the dog's ration,' he mused, 'I shall be torn to shreds by the entire pack of ferocious hounds. And if I do not produce any meat for the King's table I run the risk of being hanged. What am I to do?'

'And then,' said his wife, 'even if you got some meat it would not do to cook it in the kitchen. The smell would attract attention. You should do well to braise it, after dark, outside the town, somewhere under the bushes near the crematory.'

The chef thought over the suggestion. And towards midnight he prowled about the cremation grounds far from the city—the area known as "The Burning Ghat." There luck led him to a stray, motherless calf. He got hold of it and managed to roast it rather indifferently on a spit. At meal time this poorly roasted veal was served to Lionel with a thick sauce.

'My last hour has come,' the chef murmured to himself when he was told that the King wished to have a word with him as soon as he had risen from table. 'Lord, help me,' he prayed as he presented himself before Lionel. He could hardly believe his ears when he was warmly congratulated on his good cooking by his royal master.

'My dear man,' Lionel said, 'I must admit I have never tasted such delicious food in my life. It was simply marvellous. Its only shortcoming was the sauce. How did you manage to get the meat?'

At first the chef thought that the King was making fun of his poor cooking. He was too frightened to speak. And then, what was he to say? However, as Lionel was insistent, he fell on his knees and craved for mercy.

'Where did you get the meat from?' the King repeated his demand. 'I must have an answer.'

The chef now confessed what he had done. The animal, he contended, belonged to no one in particular and was not likely to be missed. For it was one of the bull calves usually released on the death of a pious man by his relatives as an act of piety. He realised, he added, the enormity of his crime. 'But, sire,' he ended, 'I wanted to please your majesty. Please forgive me. I know I have sinned greatly.'

'Listen, my man,' Lionel said. 'I find nothing wrong in what you have done. Only don't talk about it to any one, not even to your wife. Now tell me what animal do they release when a wicked man is hanged or impaled? Do they release a full-grown bull?'

'I believe,' the chef stammered, not yet fully recovered from his fright, 'I believe they do nothing special. They simply burn the corpse in the crematory, in the Burning Ghat outside the city.'

'What a foolish thing to do!' Lionel muttered. 'It is silly to reduce human flesh to mere cinders. However,' he added after a pause, 'however, remember, I prefer underdone steaks—the least done are the best. Don't forget.'

The chef now recalled, all of a sudden, his wife's remarks about Lionel: 'Don't forget, my dear, his foster-mother was a man-eater lioness.' What was the King driving at? Did he want half-roasted corpses for his table? Or was he perhaps longing for raw human flesh which he must have tasted at one time with his foster-mother? A feeling of revulsion came over him.

Though in Kanchi the punishment for killing a calf was the same as for murdering a child, the chef's natural instinct found it most loathsome that Lionel should suggest his getting hold of the bodies of recently executed criminals for the royal table. He barely paid any attention to the rest of the King's remarks and insinuations, and felt greatly relieved when he was accorded the permission to withdraw.

The horrified chef did not dare to breathe a word of his interview with the King to any one, not even to his wife. He fretted uneasily when he was congratulated on his good luck—his salary was now trebled. However, he nearly gave himself away when he tried to word a coherent answer to his wife's demand, 'What have you done to get this rise in your pay?'

'No man is hanged,' he stuttered, 'I told the King, during the month of the Autumn Moon.'

'What a subject to discuss! And he has trebled your salary for this precious information! Are you not keeping, my dear, something back from me? Come, let me hear the truth. What did the King say?'

'I am telling you the truth. "I don't mind," the King said, "how you get your meat; but you will be hanged the day you send me a meatless dish." That was all.'

At this his wife counselled prudence. 'A man's worst troubles start,' she said, 'when he is able to do as he likes. So be careful, my dear. And do not forget to tell the King that he must hide the bones during these meatless weeks. Otherwise,' she added, 'anything can happen. Say what you will, I don't like the idea of breaking an old custom. If people came to know about it they would revolt.'

And people did come to know about it soon afterwards. It was a lame kid that gave away the secret one early dawn: with its piteous bleatings it protested against the kidnapper and attracted the attention of the neatherds. The ravisher—the King's chef—was caught redhanded, metaphorically and literally redhanded. The nearly killed animal's blood on his hands and clothes was proof enough to establish irrefutably his guilt.

At any other time he could have got away with a light punishment, maybe, a fine or a few strokes for stealing. But the act of trying to kill a kid in cold blood during the month of the Autumn Moon demanded exemplary chastisement. The cry of alarm of the neatherds and others brought the city's watchmen to the scene and then half the city's population as well.

But for the protection given by the watchmen, the chef would have been torn limb by limb by the infuriated populace and a crime of a greater magnitude than the slaughter of a lame kid committed on the spot. 'Let us take him to the King,' the watchmen cried to appease the crowd. 'The King will give his summary judgment. You must not take the law in your hands.'

'Why not?' shouted a section of the rabble. 'We are the people. And what we decide is the law.'

'To the palace,' clamoured another section of the crowd. 'We want to know what the King says. Such a thing has never happened before.' The will of the latter prevailed.

And a vast turbulent throng, clamouring for human blood on account of a kid, surged towards the palace with the chef surrounded by a group of watchmen. They found the King eager to receive them and hear their plaint: Lionel was mounted on his fastest charger and held upright in his right hand "the Sword of Justice," the longsword.

'Where's the lawbreaker?' Lionel demanded. 'I have been told that he was caught redhanded. Where is he?'

They pushed the chef forward. Lionel grabbed him and lifted him up on his saddle, and then flourishing his longsword galloped off with the chef in the direction of the jungle where he had spent his childhood.

'The King is going to behead him,' some said, 'in the heart of the forest.'

'No,' said some others. 'He will leave the lawbreaker at the mercy of the wild animals. This is the month of the Autumn Moon and he is not the man to break an ancient tradition by shedding blood himself.'

Only the chef's wife, with wet eyes, sighed to herself, 'They will perhaps never come back together.'

'Well,' said Lionel to the chef when they were many leagues away from Kanchi, 'there is no going back for us. As you have been loyal to me I have saved you. Now take the triple oath to serve me faithfully the rest of your days.'

The chef readily took the proposed oath: he had no choice. Lionel's naked longsword was a more effective argument than the fear of being lynched by Kanchi's populace.

'Now,' Lionel said, 'I intend to install myself in the neighbourhood of Benares.'

The chef gave a sigh of relief. So, he thought, there would be no need to lead a vagrant's life. Lionel's old class-mate, Sura-Sen, was now the king of Benares. Therefore he murmured, 'Sire, I am sure, King Sura-Sen will received you with open arms.'

'He may,' Lionel muttered. 'Most likely he would love to do so and treat me as a younger brother of his. But I want to teach that prig a lesson. It was he who spoilt my days in Taxila with his fanaticism. During his entire stay at the university,' Lionel went on, 'Sura-Sen never broke a single rule. And what is still worse, he forced his college mates to follow his example.' He gritted his teeth and continued, 'If I had had some decent food in those days I should not be hankering for raw flesh now. My foster-mother was a lioness; she was a man-eater, and I want to follow her steps. Sura-Sen will be the first man I shall eat whole without, let me assure you, any of the wretched thick sauce you prepare.'

'But,' the horrified chef wondered, 'why Sura-Sen of all the people of the world?' Sura-Sen, though living in far off Benares, was renowned in Kanchi for his sterling qualities. He was a generous patron of arts and letters: he paid a hundred gold pieces to someone the chef knew—a needy bard of Kanchi —for a short poem of only four lines:

> *Where the body has a soul*
> *Love has gone before.*
> *Where no love inspires the whole,*
> *Dust it is—no more!*

This poet of Kanchi was invited to visit Benares as Sura-Sen's guest. 'So that,' Sura-Sen's letter stated, 'we may work together. Here is a stanza which recalls your own verses:

> *Loveless natures, cold and hard*
> *Live for self alone.*
> *Hearts where love abides regard*
> *Self as scarce their own.'*

'I hate prigs,' Lionel declared, bringing the chef's musings to an end. 'Sura-Sen is the biggest prig I have ever come across. That's why he shall be my very first victim. I must, however, collect ninety-nine others. He will be devoured in the presence of his ninety-nine admirers.'

'What is a prig?' the chef asked himself, but he did not dare to put the question to his master especially as the latter was now anxious to give a demonstration of his power of roaring like a lion.

The surprised man saw Lionel run about on all fours like a wild animal, his hair standing on end like the mane of an enraged lion, and his head lowered so that his lips almost touched the earth; then he heard him utter a terrifying roar that shook the ground under his feet as though it were convulsed by subterranean thunder. He felt his blood turned into water and his limbs paralysed while his heart ceased to beat. He remained riveted to the spot till the rumbling echoes of Lionel's inhuman cry and its reverberations died away.

And the chef was not the only being to experience this peculiar petrifying effect of Lionel's thunderous roar. For a deathlike stillness descended immediately on the entire area— no animal or bird dared to move or utter the least sound for a long time.

'Do you see?' said Lionel getting to his feet. 'As I was brought up on the milk of a lioness, I have the strength of a lion, and I can paralyse any man or animal with my roar; I can kill as well with my cry. Now don't try to run away from me without my permission. For it would mean your immediate recapture and sure destruction. And then, you mustn't dream of setting free any of the victims I am going to capture unless you want to be killed along with the object of your pity. Finally, remember,' he ended, 'I want you to act as my stooge. Your triple oath binds you to serve me faithfully.'

They then set out for Benares. The immense distance between Kanchi and the Holy City was covered in a comparatively short time. And soon after they had installed themselves in a forest close to Benares, Lionel said to the chef, 'Now I am ready for my hundredth captive, King Sura-Sen of Benares. You will have to go to his palace one of these days with a letter from me.'

But where were the ninety-nine unfortunate men to whom Lionel referred? The secret was soon revealed to the chef. He was brought to the brink of an immense bowl-shaped pit in the midst of the forest. 'There,' said Lionel pointing to the bottom of the pit, 'there they are: my ninety-nine captives, all great admirers of Sura-Sen. I have put them in this deep trap. Do you see them? I had to cover,' he explained, 'long distances every night—when you snored peacefully in spite of your being in fetters—in order to get hold of them. I have dumped them

137

there, some of the finest prigs of Nalanda University. They can't get out because the sides of the pit are too steep. I can, of course, haul up any of them with my lasso.'

The chef then heard from Lionel that Sura-Sen was busy celebrating the Spring Festival outside Benares, and it would be an easy task to capture him alive: for he was spending most of his time not in his palace but in a walled park.

Lionel came to know everything about Sura-Sen's movements from the letters he found on some of his captives.

'The much looked for Spring Festival is at hand,' one such letter began. 'Hurry, poet! Hurry to Benares! Come soon with your writings to the chief seat of learning in India, India's true capital. Benares is prospering under a wise ruler anxious to keep the feast with a pomp worthy of the city's wealth, culture and tradition. The season and other circumstances are propitious to the drama; the palace of King Sura-Sen is hospitable to letters. But where is a work to be found exquisite enough to satisfy the critical faculty of Sura-Sen and his court save in your home? A woman writer,' the letter went on, 'Hladini by name, has submitted a heroic comedy for the Drama Competition, and it has been hailed as a masterpiece by her friends. But, from what I have heard from others, this heroic comedy is a cheap farce compared with the least of your plays. . . .'

Another letter gave an hour-by-hour account of Sura-Sen's activities and movements, and advised the addressee to accost the King at the time of his entering the Walled Park and present him with a short poem: and that was the best means for obtaining a 'consolation prize' straightaway—a purse of gold coins.

Still another missive described the place where the Spring Festival plays were performed: 'The hall glows with subdued lights and wall-sconces; precious stones sparkle, set in the gold of the pillars and in the diadems of the princes; banners of many colours hang from the columns. The roll of drums announces the opening of a show. A chorus chants a welcome and pays homage to gods, priests, and monarchs. The director then recites the opening blessing, turns towards the wings of the stage and summons an actress, talks with her for a moment, and afterwards calls for a song to charm the audience. Then two lovely figures stationed before the curtain draw its folds apart to reveal an Apsara, a daughter of the celestial choristers, who has lost her way in a dense forest. She appears clad in a simple tunic, which at once hides and reveals her form. Her attitude, her gestures, ravish the heart and eyes, and when she speaks her voice is music. . . . The court of Sura-Sen trembles with a serene and deep emotion: a new masterpiece has just been created. . . .'

Lionel gnashed his teeth as he read these letters. 'The prig!' he muttered, 'The prig always got the better of me; but he will soon see what I can do. I will paralyse him with my roar and then drag him to the brink of the captives' pit. It would be fun to see him squirm.'

Lionel's chef presented Sura-Sen with his master's letter when he was talking to a needy poet of a foreign land near a side-entrance to the Walled Park.

'Of course,' Sura-Sen said to the poet, 'I shall hear your verses. Let me, however, see what this letter says.' His face clouded as he scanned its contents.

'May I recite my poem now?' the poet asked. 'It is a short one.'

'I am sorry to disappoint you,' Sura-Sen replied. 'My friend Lionel needs me immediately. I must go now. But I give you my word of honour that tomorrow at this place and at this very hour I shall hear your recital.' He then turned to the chef and said, 'Messenger, where is Lionel? Please take me to him at once.'

'Over there, sire,' the chef said as he pointed to a nearby bush.

And a second later a terrific roar filled the air and Lionel fell upon Sura-Sen like a thunderbolt. And before any one had realised what was happening he vanished like a flash of lightning, carrying his hundredth captive, Sura-Sen, with him.

'What was it?' they asked the chef when they had recovered their power of speech. 'Who are you?' the guards demanded. 'What was the letter you gave to King Sura-Sen? Where do you come from?'

'Oh,' the chef replied as he shrugged his shoulders, 'Oh, it was nothing extraordinary. My master is a magician. He wanted to give King Sura-Sen a demonstration of his skill. Please carry on your Festival in the usual way. He will be back here tomorrow at this hour.'

'That's what he told me,' the poet now broke in. 'He gave me his word of honour as he laid his hand on his sword. I believe the poor magician's need is greater than mine. For the King's face fell as he read the letter.'

As the guards continued their interrogation of the poet, the chef slank away unnoticed to the nearby jungle, to Lionel's lair. There on the edge of the captives' pit he found Sura-Sen with his master.

'So you are shedding tears like a woman,' Lionel taunted Sura-Sen, 'because your last hour has come! You coward! And you preach that a man should so live that he may leave the world at a moment's notice without any qualms! You are a fraud!'

'Lionel!' Sura-Sen said, 'You ought to know better. I have never shed tears for my own self, never.'

'Then for whom are these tears? For me, I presume!'

'Certainly not for you, Lionel. That I can assure you.'

In his heart of hearts Lionel felt a deep stab when Sura-Sen, instead of grovelling, jeered at his captor for trying to understand the cause of his involuntary tears. The situation now turned out to be very different from what Lionel had foreseen: though in tears Sura-Sen was not going to yield without a fight. And who could foretell the outcome of the fight?

In Taxila, Lionel reflected, they had wrestled together, not once but many, many times, and not in a single instance had the result been anything but the most complete stalemate. In their fencing matches the outcome was no different. In their games of chess it was just the same.

However, now he had, he thought, one definite advantage over Sura-Sen: that was his power of roaring. But on second thoughts he began to doubt if this was truly a real superiority, outweighing other factors. For he recalled an essay on Military Tactics by Sura-Sen, in which it was propounded: 'If the enemy attack you with shouts meet his challenge in complete silence; but when he advances in silence repel him with shouts. Stratagem, however, should be met with stratagem. Though an adversary making a sudden onslaught has the initial advantage, he reveals on the other hand his weaknesses too soon to the attacked, who should profit from his observations.' Perhaps, Lionel concluded, Sura-Sen was practising a ruse and his tears were a mere make-believe.

The more he pondered the more he became doubtful of an assured victory over his former friend, Sura-Sen. 'What would happen,' he asked himself, 'if in our hand-to-hand struggle the prig manoeuvres that we both roll down into the bottom of the pit? There instead of one to contend with I should have a hundred. And Sura-Sen's ninety-nine allies may see to it that no roar issues from my throat.'

By now the captives at the bottom of the pit had recognised their patron Sura-Sen and they raised a shout that rent the air. 'Victory to Sura-Sen!' they cried in unison. 'Victory to the Monarch of Benares! Victory to Siva's Son!'

Lionel immediately got on all fours and putting his lips close to the ground uttered one of his longest and loudest roars: the earth trembled, the trees shook, the rocks shivered; but the uproar he made, though terrific, did not drown the thunder of the paean rising from the captives' lips to the seventh heaven. 'So that's that,' Lionel said to himself. 'Now my roar has lost its terror. All that remains at present is trickery.' So turning towards Sura-Sen, he said, 'Tell me the truth, are your tears for evoking my mercy, or for throwing me off my guard?'

Sura-Sen refused to give an answer at first, but he was eventually provoked to break silence. 'Lionel,' he said, 'no man, however insane, ever craves mercy from a beast. You have reduced yourself to the status of a low beast, a ferocious animal. You know who I am: Siva's Son, King of Benares, Prince of the Holy City, Protector of the Poor, Father of the Fatherless, Bestower of Bounties, Doctor of Taxila, Regent of Nalanda. Such a man does not ask mercy of a blood-sucking hirsute brute: a brute who has forgotten the law of chivalry and uses a stooge to get hold of a monarch.'

'Then,' Lionel interrupted, 'you want to throw me off my guard!'

'Nonsense! Are wild animals thrown off their guard by human tears?'

'What is it then that makes you weep? Tell me, and I will grant you a boon: I will release you for twenty-four hours on parole. Swear on your sword as a soldier that you will come back here tomorrow at this hour, alone and unarmed.'

Sura-Sen accepted Lionel's offer. The reason for his tears was simple: 'I want to meet a needy poet from a foreign land,' Sura-Sen said. 'This poor man counts much upon my help. He has come from a distant land in the hope of succour from me. Were I to fail him he would be heart-broken.'

'Sura-Sen,' Lionel shrieked, 'You are a prig and a very low prig at that. At his last hour a man weeps over his wife, his children, his friends and relatives, over his possessions and belongings, over the warmth of life and the beauty of the day and the night. But you are such a pompous pedant that you pule over poetry when death stares you in the face. Anyway, go now and deal with your poet in your puppyish way.'

When Sura-Sen had gone Lionel thought over his own past and prayed that his friend would break his oath and fail to return to the forest. For a sense of shame humiliated him. He knew that Sura-Sen could have easily used his sword with a deadly effect when he was pounced upon in the neighbourhood of the Walled Park. Why didn't he do that? 'I never attack a needy friend,' was Sura-Sen's answer. 'I recognised you,

Lionel,' he said, 'the moment I saw you. And I felt you were in dire need of succour. Now you know the reason why I did not use my sword to ward you off.'

The next day Lionel was in a furious mood. He ate up the bark of a hundred tree trunks to calm his nerves. As this did not help him much he chased and outran the fleetest of the deer to tear them to pieces and wallow in their blood. He then turned to his chef, who thought his last hour was at hand, and administered him a kick, declaring that he was now absolved of his oath of loyalty. The poor man lay, crouching, not knowing what to do. 'Clear out,' Lionel thundered. 'Clear out, and never show your face to me. I am sick of the very sight of you.'

At this the chef got to his feet and fled in the direction of Benares.

Now Lionel sat down to compose himself. This, however, did not change his mood and he began roaring till the whole forest shook. Then in a hoarse voice he began talking aloud to himself: he started a violent debate with his former self and his present ego. This disputation led him to conclude that he was a fool. 'It was foolish of me,' he said to himself, 'to let that chef escape. He was the cause of my leaving Kanchi, and he will now undo me in Benares. I wanted to be even with Sura-Sen, but that seems to be out of the question at present. For,' he kept on, 'even if I were to eat up his very nails and hair, leaving no earthly trace whatsoever of him, he will be the acknowledged winner in the long run. All Benares will be talking of their marvellous king! Of Sura-Sen, the man of his word! A dead Sura-Sen will thus triumph over a living Lionel. Sura-Sen will be known as honourable and I as despicable—a mere treacherous man-eater. Would to God this rascally Sura-Sen would stay away from me and remain where he now happens to be in the Festival Hall, or in the green room of his favourite actresses, or in the monastery of the shaven-headed friars.'

Lionel was raving like one possessed when Sura-Sen, true to

143

his word, turned up unarmed and unattended as he had promised to do.

'Why have you come back?' Lionel snarled. 'Couldn't you leave me in peace? Must you force me to eat you up whole?'

'I want to keep my oath,' Sura-Sen replied.

'Does a man keep his oath with a hirsute beast? Didn't you call me a wild animal? Does a brute, a creature of prey, merit parleys with a king and a king of Benares at that? What has happened to your intelligence, Sura-Sen?'

'You are a beast, but not a beast beyond redemption.'

'What makes you think that?'

'Because you allowed me a respite so that I could help a needy poet.'

'Ha! Ha! The prig is talking his puppy dialect. Poets and players, pretty girls and pious priests! Well, what did your poet say?'

'Nothing that would interest you in your present mood. Poetry is of no value whatsoever to apes and lions, to beasts of prey, and to men who emulate them.'

Lionel's curiosity was pricked. He wanted to know the contents of the poem of four stanzas for which Sura-Sen had paid four hundred gold pieces that very morning. Sura-Sen on his part refused any information on this score save that the four stanzas of the bard had strengthened his faith:

> Unschooled in music, poetry, and art
> Man is a beast—a hairless, tail-less beast:
> He does not swallow grass; for this at least
> The other beasts may well be glad at heart.

'Was that what your precious bard gave you for your bag of gold?' Lionel sneered.

'No,' Sura-Sen shook his head. 'Why should I repeat his verses to you? One does not cast pearls before swine nor give what is holy to the dogs.'

'Suppose I grant you four wishes for the four stanzas,' Lionel proposed, 'will you then recite them to me?'

'On that condition, gladly.' Sura-Sen's four wishes were these: Lionel should curb the beast in him; he should set the captives free, and fully compensate for the damage he had done to them and others; and finally he must strive to lead a long and prosperous life.

'Good heavens!' Lionel cried, 'What a fool! Suppose I eat you up first and then fulfil the four conditions. What would happen then?'

Sura-Sen replied that even then he would not think of altering his four conditions. For he was not afraid of dying, as he knew he had lived tolerably well a fairly satisfactory life. Moreover, he recalled the teachings of his masters at Taxila:

> *Then greet whatever comes*
> *Of joy or grievous smart,*
> *Delight or pain, with brave*
> *Unconquerable heart.*

'After all,' Sura-Sen ended, 'every man must eat a peck of ashes before he dies. So why should I make a fuss at being devoured by the foster-son of a lioness?'

At this Lionel shot up like a lion and fell upon Sura-Sen, roaring, 'I want to be even with you.' 'That's why I am here,' Sura-Sen responded, as he received him with outstretched arms.

The two did not fight, as the ninety-nine liberated captives had at first suspected; they did not struggle nor wrestle; they held each other in close embrace, like reconciled brothers brought together after an age. For Lionel was changed into his former self as Sura-Sen whispered in his ears the four stanzas of gnomic poetry he had learnt from the bard of a distant land.

Lionel lost his animal nature entirely as well as his hirsute appearance when Sura-Sen's barber shaved his face and head. Later, in royal robes and showering largess, he went with his friend, Sura-Sen, to the Drama Festival. He was delighted to find the artistes of Kanchi well represented there. Soon the news spread that he was rivalling the King of Benares as a patron of arts and letters.

And when he returned to Kanchi he was received with rejoicings by his people. His chef, however, opted to remain in Benares and opened a pastry shop there; it was looked after by his wife, who proved to be a real blessing.

A CATALOG OF SELECTED
DOVER BOOKS
IN ALL FIELDS OF INTEREST

A CATALOG OF SELECTED DOVER
BOOKS IN ALL FIELDS OF INTEREST

CONCERNING THE SPIRITUAL IN ART, Wassily Kandinsky. Pioneering work by father of abstract art. Thoughts on color theory, nature of art. Analysis of earlier masters. 12 illustrations. 80pp. of text. 5⅜ × 8½. 23411-8 Pa. $3.95

ANIMALS: 1,419 Copyright-Free Illustrations of Mammals, Birds, Fish, Insects, etc., Jim Harter (ed.). Clear wood engravings present, in extremely lifelike poses, over 1,000 species of animals. One of the most extensive pictorial sourcebooks of its kind. Captions. Index. 284pp. 9 × 12. 23766-4 Pa. $12.95

CELTIC ART: The Methods of Construction, George Bain. Simple geometric techniques for making Celtic interlacements, spirals, Kells-type initials, animals, humans, etc. Over 500 illustrations. 160pp. 9 × 12. (USO) 22923-8 Pa. $9.95

AN ATLAS OF ANATOMY FOR ARTISTS, Fritz Schider. Most thorough reference work on art anatomy in the world. Hundreds of illustrations, including selections from works by Vesalius, Leonardo, Goya, Ingres, Michelangelo, others. 593 illustrations. 192pp. 7⅛ × 10¼. 20241-0 Pa. $9.95

CELTIC HAND STROKE-BY-STROKE (Irish Half-Uncial from "The Book of Kells"): An Arthur Baker Calligraphy Manual, Arthur Baker. Complete guide to creating each letter of the alphabet in distinctive Celtic manner. Covers hand position, strokes, pens, inks, paper, more. Illustrated. 48pp. 8¼ × 11. 24336-2 Pa. $3.95

EASY ORIGAMI, John Montroll. Charming collection of 32 projects (hat, cup, pelican, piano, swan, many more) specially designed for the novice origami hobbyist. Clearly illustrated easy-to-follow instructions insure that even beginning papercrafters will achieve successful results. 48pp. 8¼ × 11. 27298-2 Pa. $2.95

THE COMPLETE BOOK OF BIRDHOUSE CONSTRUCTION FOR WOOD-WORKERS, Scott D. Campbell. Detailed instructions, illustrations, tables. Also data on bird habitat and instinct patterns. Bibliography. 3 tables. 63 illustrations in 15 figures. 48pp. 5¼ × 8½. 24407-5 Pa. $1.95

BLOOMINGDALE'S ILLUSTRATED 1886 CATALOG: Fashions, Dry Goods and Housewares, Bloomingdale Brothers. Famed merchants' extremely rare catalog depicting about 1,700 products: clothing, housewares, firearms, dry goods, jewelry, more. Invaluable for dating, identifying vintage items. Also, copyright-free graphics for artists, designers. Co-published with Henry Ford Museum & Greenfield Village. 160pp. 8¼ × 11. 25780-0 Pa. $9.95

HISTORIC COSTUME IN PICTURES, Braun & Schneider. Over 1,450 costumed figures in clearly detailed engravings—from dawn of civilization to end of 19th century. Captions. Many folk costumes. 256pp. 8⅜ × 11¼. 23150-X Pa. $11.95

CATALOG OF DOVER BOOKS

STICKLEY CRAFTSMAN FURNITURE CATALOGS, Gustav Stickley and L. & J. G. Stickley. Beautiful, functional furniture in two authentic catalogs from 1910. 594 illustrations, including 277 photos, show settles, rockers, armchairs, reclining chairs, bookcases, desks, tables. 183pp. 6½ × 9¼.   23838-5 Pa. $9.95

AMERICAN LOCOMOTIVES IN HISTORIC PHOTOGRAPHS: 1858 to 1949, Ron Ziel (ed.). A rare collection of 126 meticulously detailed official photographs, called "builder portraits," of American locomotives that majestically chronicle the rise of steam locomotive power in America. Introduction. Detailed captions. xi + 129pp. 9 × 12.   27393-8 Pa. $12.95

AMERICA'S LIGHTHOUSES: An Illustrated History, Francis Ross Holland, Jr. Delightfully written, profusely illustrated fact-filled survey of over 200 American lighthouses since 1716. History, anecdotes, technological advances, more. 240pp. 8 × 10¾.   25576-X Pa. $11.95

TOWARDS A NEW ARCHITECTURE, Le Corbusier. Pioneering manifesto by founder of "International School." Technical and aesthetic theories, views of industry, economics, relation of form to function, "mass-production split" and much more. Profusely illustrated. 320pp. 6⅛ × 9¼. (USO)   25023-7 Pa. $9.95

HOW THE OTHER HALF LIVES, Jacob Riis. Famous journalistic record, exposing poverty and degradation of New York slums around 1900, by major social reformer. 100 striking and influential photographs. 233pp. 10 × 7⅞.
22012-5 Pa $10.95

FRUIT KEY AND TWIG KEY TO TREES AND SHRUBS, William M. Harlow. One of the handiest and most widely used identification aids. Fruit key covers 120 deciduous and evergreen species; twig key 160 deciduous species. Easily used. Over 300 photographs. 126pp. 5⅜ × 8½.   20511-8 Pa. $3.95

COMMON BIRD SONGS, Dr. Donald J. Borror. Songs of 60 most common U.S. birds: robins, sparrows, cardinals, bluejays, finches, more—arranged in order of increasing complexity. Up to 9 variations of songs of each species.
Cassette and manual 99911-4 $8.95

ORCHIDS AS HOUSE PLANTS, Rebecca Tyson Northen. Grow cattleyas and many other kinds of orchids—in a window, in a case, or under artificial light. 63 illustrations. 148pp. 5⅜ × 8½.   23261-1 Pa. $4.95

MONSTER MAZES, Dave Phillips. Masterful mazes at four levels of difficulty. Avoid deadly perils and evil creatures to find magical treasures. Solutions for all 32 exciting illustrated puzzles. 48pp. 8¼ × 11.   26005-4 Pa. $2.95

MOZART'S DON GIOVANNI (DOVER OPERA LIBRETTO SERIES), Wolfgang Amadeus Mozart. Introduced and translated by Ellen H. Bleiler. Standard Italian libretto, with complete English translation. Convenient and thoroughly portable—an ideal companion for reading along with a recording or the performance itself. Introduction. List of characters. Plot summary. 121pp. 5¼ × 8½.
24944-1 Pa. $2.95

TECHNICAL MANUAL AND DICTIONARY OF CLASSICAL BALLET, Gail Grant. Defines, explains, comments on steps, movements, poses and concepts. 15-page pictorial section. Basic book for student, viewer. 127pp. 5⅜ × 8½.
21843-0 Pa. $4.95

BRASS INSTRUMENTS: Their History and Development, Anthony Baines. Authoritative, updated survey of the evolution of trumpets, trombones, bugles, cornets, French horns, tubas and other brass wind instruments. Over 140 illustrations and 48 music examples. Corrected and updated by author. New preface. Bibliography. 320pp. 5⅜ × 8½. 27574-4 Pa. $9.95

HOLLYWOOD GLAMOR PORTRAITS, John Kobal (ed.). 145 photos from 1926–49. Harlow, Gable, Bogart, Bacall; 94 stars in all. Full background on photographers, technical aspects. 160pp. 8⅜ × 11¼. 23352-9 Pa. $11.95

MAX AND MORITZ, Wilhelm Busch. Great humor classic in both German and English. Also 10 other works: "Cat and Mouse," "Plisch and Plumm," etc. 216pp. 5⅜ × 8½. 20181-3 Pa. $5.95

THE RAVEN AND OTHER FAVORITE POEMS, Edgar Allan Poe. Over 40 of the author's most memorable poems: "The Bells," "Ulalume," "Israfel," "To Helen," "The Conqueror Worm," "Eldorado," "Annabel Lee," many more. Alphabetic lists of titles and first lines. 64pp. 5³⁄₁₆ × 8¼. 26685-0 Pa. $1.00

SEVEN SCIENCE FICTION NOVELS, H. G. Wells. The standard collection of the great novels. Complete, unabridged. First Men in the Moon, Island of Dr. Moreau, War of the Worlds, Food of the Gods, Invisible Man, Time Machine, In the Days of the Comet. Total of 1,015pp. 5⅜ × 8½. (USO) 20264-X Clothbd. $29.95

AMULETS AND SUPERSTITIONS, E. A. Wallis Budge. Comprehensive discourse on origin, powers of amulets in many ancient cultures: Arab, Persian, Babylonian, Assyrian, Egyptian, Gnostic, Hebrew, Phoenician, Syriac, etc. Covers cross, swastika, crucifix, seals, rings, stones, etc. 584pp. 5⅜ × 8½. 23573-4 Pa. $12.95

RUSSIAN STORIES/PYCCKNE PACCKA3bl: A Dual-Language Book, edited by Gleb Struve. Twelve tales by such masters as Chekhov, Tolstoy, Dostoevsky, Pushkin, others. Excellent word-for-word English translations on facing pages, plus teaching and study aids, Russian/English vocabulary, biographical/critical introductions, more. 416pp. 5⅜ × 8½. 26244-8 Pa. $8.95

PHILADELPHIA THEN AND NOW: 60 Sites Photographed in the Past and Present, Kenneth Finkel and Susan Oyama. Rare photographs of City Hall, Logan Square, Independence Hall, Betsy Ross House, other landmarks juxtaposed with contemporary views. Captures changing face of historic city. Introduction. Captions. 128pp. 8¼ × 11. 25790-8 Pa. $9.95

AIA ARCHITECTURAL GUIDE TO NASSAU AND SUFFOLK COUNTIES, LONG ISLAND, The American Institute of Architects, Long Island Chapter, and the Society for the Preservation of Long Island Antiquities. Comprehensive, well-researched and generously illustrated volume brings to life over three centuries of Long Island's great architectural heritage. More than 240 photographs with authoritative, extensively detailed captions. 176pp. 8¼ × 11. 26946-9 Pa. $14.95

NORTH AMERICAN INDIAN LIFE: Customs and Traditions of 23 Tribes, Elsie Clews Parsons (ed.). 27 fictionalized essays by noted anthropologists examine religion, customs, government, additional facets of life among the Winnebago, Crow, Zuni, Eskimo, other tribes. 480pp. 6⅛ × 9¼. 27377-6 Pa. $10.95

CATALOG OF DOVER BOOKS

FRANK LLOYD WRIGHT'S HOLLYHOCK HOUSE, Donald Hoffmann. Lavishly illustrated, carefully documented study of one of Wright's most controversial residential designs. Over 120 photographs, floor plans, elevations, etc. Detailed perceptive text by noted Wright scholar. Index. 128pp. 9¼ × 10¾.
27133-1 Pa. $11.95

THE MALE AND FEMALE FIGURE IN MOTION: 60 Classic Photographic Sequences, Eadweard Muybridge. 60 true-action photographs of men and women walking, running, climbing, bending, turning, etc., reproduced from rare 19th-century masterpiece. vi + 121pp. 9 × 12.
24745-7 Pa. $10.95

1001 QUESTIONS ANSWERED ABOUT THE SEASHORE, N. J. Berrill and Jacquelyn Berrill. Queries answered about dolphins, sea snails, sponges, starfish, fishes, shore birds, many others. Covers appearance, breeding, growth, feeding, much more. 305pp. 5¼ × 8¼.
23366-9 Pa. $7.95

GUIDE TO OWL WATCHING IN NORTH AMERICA, Donald S. Heintzelman. Superb guide offers complete data and descriptions of 19 species: barn owl, screech owl, snowy owl, many more. Expert coverage of owl-watching equipment, conservation, migrations and invasions, etc. Guide to observing sites. 84 illustrations. xiii + 193pp. 5⅜ × 8½.
27344-X Pa. $8.95

MEDICINAL AND OTHER USES OF NORTH AMERICAN PLANTS: A Historical Survey with Special Reference to the Eastern Indian Tribes, Charlotte Erichsen-Brown. Chronological historical citations document 500 years of usage of plants, trees, shrubs native to eastern Canada, northeastern U.S. Also complete identifying information. 343 illustrations. 544pp. 6½ × 9¼.
25951-X Pa. $12.95

STORYBOOK MAZES, Dave Phillips. 23 stories and mazes on two-page spreads: Wizard of Oz, Treasure Island, Robin Hood, etc. Solutions. 64pp. 8¼ × 11.
23628-5 Pa. $2.95

NEGRO FOLK MUSIC, U.S.A., Harold Courlander. Noted folklorist's scholarly yet readable analysis of rich and varied musical tradition. Includes authentic versions of over 40 folk songs. Valuable bibliography and discography. xi + 324pp. 5⅜ × 8½.
27350-4 Pa. $7.95

MOVIE-STAR PORTRAITS OF THE FORTIES, John Kobal (ed.). 163 glamor, studio photos of 106 stars of the 1940s: Rita Hayworth, Ava Gardner, Marlon Brando, Clark Gable, many more. 176pp. 8⅜ × 11¼.
23546-7 Pa. $11.95

BENCHLEY LOST AND FOUND, Robert Benchley. Finest humor from early 30s, about pet peeves, child psychologists, post office and others. Mostly unavailable elsewhere. 73 illustrations by Peter Arno and others. 183pp. 5⅜ × 8½.
22410-4 Pa. $5.95

YEKL and THE IMPORTED BRIDEGROOM AND OTHER STORIES OF YIDDISH NEW YORK, Abraham Cahan. Film Hester Street based on Yekl (1896). Novel, other stories among first about Jewish immigrants on N.Y.'s East Side. 240pp. 5⅜ × 8½.
22427-9 Pa. $6.95

SELECTED POEMS, Walt Whitman. Generous sampling from *Leaves of Grass.* Twenty-four poems include "I Hear America Singing," "Song of the Open Road," "I Sing the Body Electric," "When Lilacs Last in the Dooryard Bloom'd," "O Captain! My Captain!"—all reprinted from an authoritative edition. Lists of titles and first lines. 128pp. 5³⁄₁₆ × 8¼.
26878-0 Pa. $1.00

THE BEST TALES OF HOFFMANN, E. T. A. Hoffmann. 10 of Hoffmann's most important stories: "Nutcracker and the King of Mice," "The Golden Flowerpot," etc. 458pp. 5⅜ × 8½. 21793-0 Pa. $8.95

FROM FETISH TO GOD IN ANCIENT EGYPT, E. A. Wallis Budge. Rich detailed survey of Egyptian conception of "God" and gods, magic, cult of animals, Osiris, more. Also, superb English translations of hymns and legends. 240 illustrations. 545pp. 5⅜ × 8½. 25803-3 Pa. $11.95

FRENCH STORIES/CONTES FRANÇAIS: A Dual-Language Book, Wallace Fowlie. Ten stories by French masters, Voltaire to Camus: "Micromegas" by Voltaire; "The Atheist's Mass" by Balzac; "Minuet" by de Maupassant; "The Guest" by Camus, six more. Excellent English translations on facing pages. Also French-English vocabulary list, exercises, more. 352pp. 5⅜ × 8½. 26443-2 Pa. $8.95

CHICAGO AT THE TURN OF THE CENTURY IN PHOTOGRAPHS: 122 Historic Views from the Collections of the Chicago Historical Society, Larry A. Viskochil. Rare large-format prints offer detailed views of City Hall, State Street, the Loop, Hull House, Union Station, many other landmarks, circa 1904–1913. Introduction. Captions. Maps. 144pp. 9⅜ × 12¼. 24656-6 Pa. $12.95

OLD BROOKLYN IN EARLY PHOTOGRAPHS, 1865–1929, William Lee Younger. Luna Park, Gravesend race track, construction of Grand Army Plaza, moving of Hotel Brighton, etc. 157 previously unpublished photographs. 165pp. 8⅞ × 11¾. 23587-4 Pa. $13.95

THE MYTHS OF THE NORTH AMERICAN INDIANS, Lewis Spence. Rich anthology of the myths and legends of the Algonquins, Iroquois, Pawnees and Sioux, prefaced by an extensive historical and ethnological commentary. 36 illustrations. 480pp. 5⅜ × 8½. 25967-6 Pa. $8.95

AN ENCYCLOPEDIA OF BATTLES: Accounts of Over 1,560 Battles from 1479 B.C. to the Present, David Eggenberger. Essential details of every major battle in recorded history from the first battle of Megiddo in 1479 B.C. to Grenada in 1984. List of Battle Maps. New Appendix covering the years 1967–1984. Index. 99 illustrations. 544pp. 6½ × 9¼. 24913-1 Pa. $14.95

SAILING ALONE AROUND THE WORLD, Captain Joshua Slocum. First man to sail around the world, alone, in small boat. One of great feats of seamanship told in delightful manner. 67 illustrations. 294pp. 5⅜ × 8½. 20326-3 Pa. $5.95

ANARCHISM AND OTHER ESSAYS, Emma Goldman. Powerful, penetrating, prophetic essays on direct action, role of minorities, prison reform, puritan hypocrisy, violence, etc. 271pp. 5⅜ × 8½. 22484-8 Pa. $5.95

MYTHS OF THE HINDUS AND BUDDHISTS, Ananda K. Coomaraswamy and Sister Nivedita. Great stories of the epics; deeds of Krishna, Shiva, taken from puranas, Vedas, folk tales; etc. 32 illustrations. 400pp. 5⅜ × 8½. 21759-0 Pa. $9.95

BEYOND PSYCHOLOGY, Otto Rank. Fear of death, desire of immortality, nature of sexuality, social organization, creativity, according to Rankian system. 291pp. 5⅜ × 8½. 20485-5 Pa. $8.95

A THEOLOGICO-POLITICAL TREATISE, Benedict Spinoza. Also contains unfinished Political Treatise. Great classic on religious liberty, theory of government on common consent. R. Elwes translation. Total of 421pp. 5⅜ × 8½. 20249-6 Pa. $8.95

CATALOG OF DOVER BOOKS

MY BONDAGE AND MY FREEDOM, Frederick Douglass. Born a slave, Douglass became outspoken force in antislavery movement. The best of Douglass' autobiographies. Graphic description of slave life. 464pp. 5⅜ × 8½.   22457-0 Pa. $8.95

FOLLOWING THE EQUATOR: A Journey Around the World, Mark Twain. Fascinating humorous account of 1897 voyage to Hawaii, Australia, India, New Zealand, etc. Ironic, bemused reports on peoples, customs, climate, flora and fauna, politics, much more. 197 illustrations. 720pp. 5⅜ × 8½.   26113-1 Pa. $15.95

THE PEOPLE CALLED SHAKERS, Edward D. Andrews. Definitive study of Shakers: origins, beliefs, practices, dances, social organization, furniture and crafts, etc. 33 illustrations. 351pp. 5⅜ × 8½.   21081-2 Pa. $8.95

THE MYTHS OF GREECE AND ROME, H. A. Guerber. A classic of mythology, generously illustrated, long prized for its simple, graphic, accurate retelling of the principal myths of Greece and Rome, and for its commentary on their origins and significance. With 64 illustrations by Michelangelo, Raphael, Titian, Rubens, Canova, Bernini and others. 480pp. 5⅜ × 8½.   27584-1 Pa. $9.95

PSYCHOLOGY OF MUSIC, Carl E. Seashore. Classic work discusses music as a medium from psychological viewpoint. Clear treatment of physical acoustics, auditory apparatus, sound perception, development of musical skills, nature of musical feeling, host of other topics. 88 figures. 408pp. 5⅜ × 8½. 21851-1 Pa. $9.95

THE PHILOSOPHY OF HISTORY, Georg W. Hegel. Great classic of Western thought develops concept that history is not chance but rational process, the evolution of freedom. 457pp. 5⅜ × 8½.   20112-0 Pa. $9.95

THE BOOK OF TEA, Kakuzo Okakura. Minor classic of the Orient: entertaining, charming explanation, interpretation of traditional Japanese culture in terms of tea ceremony. 94pp. 5⅜ × 8½.   20070-1 Pa. $3.95

LIFE IN ANCIENT EGYPT, Adolf Erman. Fullest, most thorough, detailed older account with much not in more recent books, domestic life, religion, magic, medicine, commerce, much more. Many illustrations reproduce tomb paintings, carvings, hieroglyphs, etc. 597pp. 5⅜ × 8½.   22632-8 Pa. $10.95

SUNDIALS, Their Theory and Construction, Albert Waugh. Far and away the best, most thorough coverage of ideas, mathematics concerned, types, construction, adjusting anywhere. Simple, nontechnical treatment allows even children to build several of these dials. Over 100 illustrations. 230pp. 5⅜ × 8½.   22947-5 Pa. $7.95

DYNAMICS OF FLUIDS IN POROUS MEDIA, Jacob Bear. For advanced students of ground water hydrology, soil mechanics and physics, drainage and irrigation engineering, and more. 335 illustrations. Exercises, with answers. 784pp. 6⅛ × 9¼.   65675-6 Pa. $19.95

SONGS OF EXPERIENCE: Facsimile Reproduction with 26 Plates in Full Color, William Blake. 26 full-color plates from a rare 1826 edition. Includes "The Tyger," "London," "Holy Thursday," and other poems. Printed text of poems. 48pp. 5¼ × 7.   24636-1 Pa. $4.95

OLD-TIME VIGNETTES IN FULL COLOR, Carol Belanger Grafton (ed.). Over 390 charming, often sentimental illustrations, selected from archives of Victorian graphics—pretty women posing, children playing, food, flowers, kittens and puppies, smiling cherubs, birds and butterflies, much more. All copyright-free. 48pp. 9¼ × 12¼.   27269-9 Pa. $5.95

PERSPECTIVE FOR ARTISTS, Rex Vicat Cole. Depth, perspective of sky and sea, shadows, much more, not usually covered. 391 diagrams, 81 reproductions of drawings and paintings. 279pp. 5⅜ × 8½. 22487-2 Pa. $6.95

DRAWING THE LIVING FIGURE, Joseph Sheppard. Innovative approach to artistic anatomy focuses on specifics of surface anatomy, rather than muscles and bones. Over 170 drawings of live models in front, back and side views, and in widely varying poses. Accompanying diagrams. 177 illustrations. Introduction. Index. 144pp. 8⅜ × 11¼. 26723-7 Pa. $8.95

GOTHIC AND OLD ENGLISH ALPHABETS: 100 Complete Fonts, Dan X. Solo. Add power, elegance to posters, signs, other graphics with 100 stunning copyright-free alphabets: Blackstone, Dolbey, Germania, 97 more—including many lower-case, numerals, punctuation marks. 104pp. 8⅛ × 11. 24695-7 Pa. $8.95

HOW TO DO BEADWORK, Mary White. Fundamental book on craft from simple projects to five-bead chains and woven works. 106 illustrations. 142pp. 5⅜ × 8. 20697-1 Pa. $4.95

THE BOOK OF WOOD CARVING, Charles Marshall Sayers. Finest book for beginners discusses fundamentals and offers 34 designs. "Absolutely first rate . . . well thought out and well executed."—E. J. Tangerman. 118pp. 7¾ × 10⅝. 23654-4 Pa. $5.95

ILLUSTRATED CATALOG OF CIVIL WAR MILITARY GOODS: Union Army Weapons, Insignia, Uniform Accessories, and Other Equipment, Schuyler, Hartley, and Graham. Rare, profusely illustrated 1846 catalog includes Union Army uniform and dress regulations, arms and ammunition, coats, insignia, flags, swords, rifles, etc. 226 illustrations. 160pp. 9 × 12. 24939-5 Pa. $10.95

WOMEN'S FASHIONS OF THE EARLY 1900s: An Unabridged Republication of "New York Fashions, 1909," National Cloak & Suit Co. Rare catalog of mail-order fashions documents women's and children's clothing styles shortly after the turn of the century. Captions offer full descriptions, prices. Invaluable resource for fashion, costume historians. Approximately 725 illustrations. 128pp. 8⅜ × 11¼. 27276-1 Pa. $11.95

THE 1912 AND 1915 GUSTAV STICKLEY FURNITURE CATALOGS, Gustav Stickley. With over 200 detailed illustrations and descriptions, these two catalogs are essential reading and reference materials and identification guides for Stickley furniture. Captions cite materials, dimensions and prices. 112pp. 6½ × 9¼. 26676-1 Pa. $9.95

EARLY AMERICAN LOCOMOTIVES, John H. White, Jr. Finest locomotive engravings from early 19th century: historical (1804–74), main-line (after 1870), special, foreign, etc. 147 plates. 142pp. 11⅜ × 8¼. 22772-3 Pa. $10.95

THE TALL SHIPS OF TODAY IN PHOTOGRAPHS, Frank O. Braynard. Lavishly illustrated tribute to nearly 100 majestic contemporary sailing vessels: Amerigo Vespucci, Clearwater, Constitution, Eagle, Mayflower, Sea Cloud, Victory, many more. Authoritative captions provide statistics, background on each ship. 190 black-and-white photographs and illustrations. Introduction. 128pp. 8⅞ × 11¾. 27163-3 Pa. $13.95

CATALOG OF DOVER BOOKS

EARLY NINETEENTH-CENTURY CRAFTS AND TRADES, Peter Stockham (ed.). Extremely rare 1807 volume describes to youngsters the crafts and trades of the day: brickmaker, weaver, dressmaker, bookbinder, ropemaker, saddler, many more. Quaint prose, charming illustrations for each craft. 20 black-and-white line illustrations. 192pp. 4⅝ × 6. 27293-1 Pa. $4.95

VICTORIAN FASHIONS AND COSTUMES FROM HARPER'S BAZAR, 1867–1898, Stella Blum (ed.). Day costumes, evening wear, sports clothes, shoes, hats, other accessories in over 1,000 detailed engravings. 320pp. 9⅜ × 12¼.
22990-4 Pa. $13.95

GUSTAV STICKLEY, THE CRAFTSMAN, Mary Ann Smith. Superb study surveys broad scope of Stickley's achievement, especially in architecture. Design philosophy, rise and fall of the Craftsman empire, descriptions and floor plans for many Craftsman houses, more. 86 black-and-white halftones. 31 line illustrations. Introduction. 208pp. 6½ × 9¼. 27210-9 Pa. $9.95

THE LONG ISLAND RAIL ROAD IN EARLY PHOTOGRAPHS, Ron Ziel. Over 220 rare photos, informative text document origin (1844) and development of rail service on Long Island. Vintage views of early trains, locomotives, stations, passengers, crews, much more. Captions. 8⅞ × 11¾. 26301-0 Pa. $13.95

THE BOOK OF OLD SHIPS: From Egyptian Galleys to Clipper Ships, Henry B. Culver. Superb, authoritative history of sailing vessels, with 80 magnificent line illustrations. Galley, bark, caravel, longship, whaler, many more. Detailed, informative text on each vessel by noted naval historian. Introduction. 256pp. 5⅜ × 8½. 27332-6 Pa. $6.95

TEN BOOKS ON ARCHITECTURE, Vitruvius. The most important book ever written on architecture. Early Roman aesthetics, technology, classical orders, site selection, all other aspects. Morgan translation. 331pp. 5⅜ × 8½. 20645-9 Pa. $8.95

THE HUMAN FIGURE IN MOTION, Eadweard Muybridge. More than 4,500 stopped-action photos, in action series, showing undraped men, women, children jumping, lying down, throwing, sitting, wrestling, carrying, etc. 390pp. 7⅞ × 10⅝.
20204-6 Clothbd. $24.95

TREES OF THE EASTERN AND CENTRAL UNITED STATES AND CANADA, William M. Harlow. Best one-volume guide to 140 trees. Full descriptions, woodlore, range, etc. Over 600 illustrations. Handy size. 288pp. 4½ × 6⅜.
20395-6 Pa. $5.95

SONGS OF WESTERN BIRDS, Dr. Donald J. Borror. Complete song and call repertoire of 60 western species, including flycatchers, juncoes, cactus wrens, many more—includes fully illustrated booklet. Cassette and manual 99913-0 $8.95

GROWING AND USING HERBS AND SPICES, Milo Miloradovich. Versatile handbook provides all the information needed for cultivation and use of all the herbs and spices available in North America. 4 illustrations. Index. Glossary. 236pp. 5⅜ × 8½. 25058-X Pa. $6.95

BIG BOOK OF MAZES AND LABYRINTHS, Walter Shepherd. 50 mazes and labyrinths in all—classical, solid, ripple, and more—in one great volume. Perfect inexpensive puzzler for clever youngsters. Full solutions. 112pp. 8⅛ × 11.
22951-3 Pa. $4.95

PIANO TUNING, J. Cree Fischer. Clearest, best book for beginner, amateur. Simple repairs, raising dropped notes, tuning by easy method of flattened fifths. No previous skills needed. 4 illustrations. 201pp. 5⅜ × 8½. 23267-0 Pa. $5.95

A SOURCE BOOK IN THEATRICAL HISTORY, A. M. Nagler. Contemporary observers on acting, directing, make-up, costuming, stage props, machinery, scene design, from Ancient Greece to Chekhov. 611pp. 5⅜ × 8½. 20515-0 Pa. $11.95

THE COMPLETE NONSENSE OF EDWARD LEAR, Edward Lear. All nonsense limericks, zany alphabets, Owl and Pussycat, songs, nonsense botany, etc., illustrated by Lear. Total of 320pp. 5⅜ × 8½. (USO) 20167-8 Pa. $6.95

VICTORIAN PARLOUR POETRY: An Annotated Anthology, Michael R. Turner. 117 gems by Longfellow, Tennyson, Browning, many lesser-known poets. "The Village Blacksmith," "Curfew Must Not Ring Tonight," "Only a Baby Small," dozens more, often difficult to find elsewhere. Index of poets, titles, first lines. xxiii + 325pp. 5⅜ × 8¼. 27044-0 Pa. $8.95

DUBLINERS, James Joyce. Fifteen stories offer vivid, tightly focused observations of the lives of Dublin's poorer classes. At least one, "The Dead," is considered a masterpiece. Reprinted complete and unabridged from standard edition. 160pp. 5³⁄₁₆ × 8¼. 26870-5 Pa. $1.00

THE HAUNTED MONASTERY and THE CHINESE MAZE MURDERS, Robert van Gulik. Two full novels by van Gulik, set in 7th-century China, continue adventures of Judge Dee and his companions. An evil Taoist monastery, seemingly supernatural events; overgrown topiary maze hides strange crimes. 27 illustrations. 328pp. 5⅜ × 8½. 23502-5 Pa. $7.95

THE BOOK OF THE SACRED MAGIC OF ABRAMELIN THE MAGE, translated by S. MacGregor Mathers. Medieval manuscript of ceremonial magic. Basic document in Aleister Crowley, Golden Dawn groups. 268pp. 5⅜ × 8½. 23211-5 Pa. $8.95

NEW RUSSIAN-ENGLISH AND ENGLISH-RUSSIAN DICTIONARY, M. A. O'Brien. This is a remarkably handy Russian dictionary, containing a surprising amount of information, including over 70,000 entries. 366pp. 4½ × 6⅛. 20208-9 Pa. $9.95

HISTORIC HOMES OF THE AMERICAN PRESIDENTS, Second, Revised Edition, Irvin Haas. A traveler's guide to American Presidential homes, most open to the public, depicting and describing homes occupied by every American President from George Washington to George Bush. With visiting hours, admission charges, travel routes. 175 photographs. Index. 160pp. 8¼ × 11. 26751-2 Pa. $10.95

NEW YORK IN THE FORTIES, Andreas Feininger. 162 brilliant photographs by the well-known photographer, formerly with *Life* magazine. Commuters, shoppers, Times Square at night, much else from city at its peak. Captions by John von Hartz. 181pp. 9¼ × 10¾. 23585-8 Pa. $12.95

INDIAN SIGN LANGUAGE, William Tomkins. Over 525 signs developed by Sioux and other tribes. Written instructions and diagrams. Also 290 pictographs. 111pp. 6⅛ × 9¼. 22029-X Pa. $3.50

THE INFLUENCE OF SEA POWER UPON HISTORY, 1660-1783, A. T. Mahan. Influential classic of naval history and tactics still used as text in war colleges. First paperback edition. 4 maps. 24 battle plans. 640pp. 5⅜ × 8½.
25509-3 Pa. $12.95

THE STORY OF THE TITANIC AS TOLD BY ITS SURVIVORS, Jack Winocour (ed.). What it was really like. Panic, despair, shocking inefficiency, and a little heroism. More thrilling than any fictional account. 26 illustrations. 320pp. 5⅜ × 8½.
20610-6 Pa. $8.95

FAIRY AND FOLK TALES OF THE IRISH PEASANTRY, William Butler Yeats (ed.). Treasury of 64 tales from the twilight world of Celtic myth and legend: "The Soul Cages," "The Kildare Pooka," "King O'Toole and his Goose," many more. Introduction and Notes by W. B. Yeats. 352pp. 5⅜ × 8½. 26941-8 Pa. $8.95

BUDDHIST MAHAYANA TEXTS, E. B. Cowell and Others (eds.). Superb, accurate translations of basic documents in Mahayana Buddhism, highly important in history of religions. The Buddha-karita of Asvaghosha, Larger Sukhavativyuha, more. 448pp. 5⅜ × 8½. 25552-2 Pa. $9.95

ONE TWO THREE . . . INFINITY: Facts and Speculations of Science, George Gamow. Great physicist's fascinating, readable overview of contemporary science: number theory, relativity, fourth dimension, entropy, genes, atomic structure, much more. 128 illustrations. Index. 352pp. 5⅜ × 8½. 25664-2 Pa. $8.95

ENGINEERING IN HISTORY, Richard Shelton Kirby, et al. Broad, nontechnical survey of history's major technological advances: birth of Greek science, industrial revolution, electricity and applied science, 20th-century automation, much more. 181 illustrations. ". . . excellent . . ."—Isis. Bibliography. vii + 530pp. 5⅜ × 8¼.
26412-2 Pa. $14.95

Prices subject to change without notice.

Available at your book dealer or write for free catalog to Dept. GI, Dover Publications, Inc., 31 East 2nd St., Mineola, N.Y. 11501. Dover publishes more than 500 books each year on science, elementary and advanced mathematics, biology, music, art, literary history, social sciences and other areas.